To Michel

Loal of love

Frank

[signature]

743-4646

Let There Be
Love

by Arend Wieman

National Library of Canada Cataloguing in Publication Data

Wieman, Arend
       Let there be love / Arend Wieman.
ISBN 1-4120-0120-X
       I. Title.
PS8595.I53144L48 2003   C813'.54   C2003-901629-3
PR9199.3.W472L48 2003

TRAFFORD

This book was published *on-demand* in cooperation with Trafford Publishing. On-demand publishing is a unique process and service of making a book available for retail sale to the public taking advantage of on-demand manufacturing and Internet marketing. **On-demand publishing** includes promotions, retail sales, manufacturing, order fulfilment, accounting and collecting royalties on behalf of the author.

Suite 6E, 2333 Government St., Victoria, B.C. V8T 4P4, CANADA
Phone   250-383-6864   Toll-free   1-888-232-4444 (Canada & US)
Fax   250-383-6804   E-mail   sales@trafford.com
Web site   www.trafford.com   TRAFFORD PUBLISHING IS A DIVISION OF TRAFFORD
HOLDINGS LTD.
Trafford Catalogue #03-0483   www.trafford.com/robots/03-0483.html

10   9   8   7   6   5   4   3   2

Let There Be Love
by Arend Wieman
Table of Contents

Let There Be Love
Prologue:

What is man's biggest handicap and often enough his downfall also? It's his vanity! Of all the passions, it is the most destructive. In general, women are not endowed with this, what one might call manly egotism. If one finds a bunch of happy people together where love is the dominant factor, women do outclass men.

The foregoing comes to bear in this novel, "Let There Be Love", where a 59-year-old man 'chances' upon five happy women — all divorcees. His spiritual exploits and age have mellowed his passions — that of the world of man. To his surprise he discovers a closeness to the ladies — all more than half his age — he never experienced before toward the opposite sex. They accept him into their midst because — instinctively perhaps — they discover that he too has their virtuous qualities. The main ingredient in their relationship is love, that of heart and soul.

The mother of three falls deeply in love with the much older man, and the three children simply love their new father.

During a flight from the Czech Republic to Germany, the plane is blown up by a terrorist, but the man of this story survives the crash, together with more than half of the passengers. Not too far hence, the mother of the three children is badly wounded during a rocket attack in Israel, while riding a sightseeing bus.

What forces are at work behind the scenes to let this happen? Or are they only accidents? Believers in the workings of karma and the Law of Cause and Effect, vital questions come to the surface and are discussed...

However, in spite of those negative happenings — with their love and spiritual beliefs — the participants in this novel are great survivors.

Chapter 1
"Bon Appétit, Ladies!"

Andrew Herden, a fair-looking man of fifty-nine and five feet eleven inches in height, was riding his mountain bicycle along one of the many logging roads in the forest. It was not too far from his home in Cobble Hill, a bit north of Victoria on Vancouver Island. Although November already, the unobstructed sun had made it a warm day near the fifty degree mark, and after an early lunch, this nature lover was on the way on top of his two-wheeler.

With the unstable world situation, particularly after the terrible 11th of September New York incident, early retirement suggestions had gone out by the government, where he had had a steady job as an Engineer. Well, financially secure, Andrew Herden had wasted no time taking the hint, and now had all day ... all week to himself. He would not make the same mistake as some of his peers did, and go fishing and loafing around. So he filled his time with biking, hiking and swimming; and, of course, there was his well-equipped workshop, where one could find him on very rainy days, building all kinds of gadgets.

1

Andrew knew all the forest roads, trails, rivers, lakes and of late the newly-established Trans-Canada Trail, the former railroad tracks to Cowichan Lake one way, and south to Victoria the other way.

Hearing some voices made him get off his vehicle and walk toward a clearing, where he encountered five ladies sitting in the grass and having their lunch. Laughing, he greeted them with: "Bon appétit, ladies!"

One of them answered, "Ach, a gentleman ..."

"Well," Andrew countered laughing, "we can't say it in English, so we say it in French ... or German ..."

"Sit down," one of them gestured, "and join us. It's all dark bread."

While sitting down, he couldn't help saying with a grin, "I never would refuse to join five young ladies, but already had my lunch an hour ago." Then he continued in the same friendly vein, "Now I have an idea why I kind of hurried to be on my way with the bike. Some invisible force no doubt had you ladies in mind, ha, ha ..."

They all began to laugh and one of them said, "You are some flatterer ..."

More serious now, but still smiling, Andrew replied, "Perhaps it sounded like that, but flattery was not on my mind, in fact I detest it. No, ladies, perhaps I shouldn't have said it in the laughing manner ... it gave the wrong impression."

A moment later then, to amend what he had suggested so lightheartedly, he explained, "You see, I do believe in a force or Spirit and at times am led on by It ... Well, in this ... in our case I might've drawn the wrong conclusion." More embarrassed than anything else, his fidgety hands and fingers played with some grass blades.

This might've gone on for half a minute, when one of the ladies stood up, held out her hand to him and said, "My name is Hety."

Getting up, Andrew replied, "I'm Andrew," and he shook her strong hand. "I guess here in nature we're only going by first names."

Then Hety said, "Don't feel bad please, it was nothing but a misunderstanding. You know what makes us five such close-knit friends? The very same you spoke about. We also believe in the guidance of Spirit and often go by our intuition."

Relaxed again, Andrew showed his old grin once more and ventured by saying, "All five of you, how extraordinary ..." Continuing then, "Mind if I shake the hand of each of you?"

After he had made the rounds from Mira to Honey to Angela and Getta, he laughed, "It's good you're only five ..." shaking his hand as if in pain, "but I loved it."

All sitting on the grass again, Andrew wondered, "How did you five ladies find each other? I mean, you're not living in the same house, or?"

Hety, who seemed to be their speaker, answered, "That's simple, we all are single again ... having had some negative experiences with the opposite sex... So we found each other and discovered we all had so much in common. As if an invisible hand had put us together."

Andrew, with a guttural laugh, couldn't help saying, "And I had to be at least twenty years your senior..." he breathed deeply. "The story of my life.

I'm always much older when I meet a nice lady... And now five of you, ha, ha. I wonder what the message is in this? Stay away from the opposite sex...," he laughed again. Then he added, "But I haven't got the discipline to simply turn a blind eye."

They all had a hearty laugh. Then Hety coaxed them to their feet by saying, "We wanted to ride our bikes for obvious reasons," and she pointed to her haunches. "So, let's be on the way. You can join us, Andrew, if you wish, so we can learn more about you, here and there."

Before they mounted their bikes, Honey couldn't help saying to their new companion, "By the way, my ex ... was much older." That remark had them all laughing again.

Often they heard Getta, riding in the back of the ladies, and Andrew holding the tail of the six riders, laughing loud, which made them all wonder what they were conversing about.

When they came to a steep incline, Hety was able to get them all close together, while pushing their vehicles, and she said with some pretended seriousness, "If we want to get to Oliphant Lake today, you two guys in the back have to stop what you're doing, making us all wonder what funny things are happening there... It slows us down too much."

Raising an arm, Andrew said grinning, "All right, sergeant..." his smirky expression said the rest. "From now on I shall put all my work into the two legs of mine and let my mouth rest in peace."

After they had stopped laughing, he suggested, "You want me to take the lead?"

With a hidden grin, Hety replied, "We'll get there

early enough, you stay right there and let silence be your guide."

Andrew had the last word, "Well said, Madam, how can I not observe such wise words."

Hety raised a hand and waved a finger at him, which could've had several meanings. It made him realize to be on guard and observe good ethics.

It amazed Andrew how much the five ladies looked alike. They all had short, fair hair. All were slender, but big busted. All seemed to have the same height of five-feet-ten or so. The exception was Honey, who was half a foot shorter.

When they came to a fork at the north end of Lake Oliphant and had dismounted to decide which way to go, Hety explained, "To the right we only have to walk a short distance and then ride our bikes again. To the left it's all walking 'til we come to the road. What do you say girls?"

Angela looked at Andrew and said, "You're so quiet now ... What do you think, Andrew?"

"Well," he began with a grin, "this is a mild year with only a little rain, so we might do all right going right. I've been that way several times and a short stretch was flooded, even too deep for a bike to ride through. This year it might be OK."

Hety suggested, "Let's not get wet and go left."

"Let's vote, we always do," Mira proposed.

They all decided to go left. Hety asked Andrew, "What about you? I didn't hear a word from you."

He replied with a grin, "You five are the old 'gang', so to speak. You hardly know me, so I just tag along. I don't mind to be over-voted by five nice ladies."

"Ho ho, ha ha," they all laughed, "listen to him..."

one of them said.

With a smirk he implied, "If you know me long enough some day, you might want to accept me as an equal partner on your forest ventures. Until then it might be better this old guy doesn't say too much. You did rather well without me."

Mira raised the question, "How do we get to know you?"

Andrew replied with his old guttural laugh, "Be patient, madam, be patient." It made them all laugh because that answer could've had several meanings.

When they came to a large, bare rock, Andrew explained, "In the heat of summer, I take a dip here at times. With you ladies present it would be a no-no, of course, unless none of you minded ... as nature created us."

"We'll bring our bathing suits," Getta suggested.

Andrew laughed, "You mean you'll take your bathing suits every time? When you start off it's probably cool and up here it's hot... You do such things on the spur of the moment rather."

Getta replied with a somber voice, "I wouldn't get undressed in front of you..."

Andrew couldn't resist saying, "It looks like you ladies have to bring your bathing ... whatever you're wearing. By the way, I go swimming often four times a week in Duncan, where we also have a hot pool. There we have to wear something, of course," he added with a smirky grin.

They all looked at him to see how he had meant it, and he thought, 'Let them do their own thinking, they'll find out soon enough how serious I am, if I am, ha, ha!"

The path around the lake was strictly for walking and rather easy to push their bikes. At one point, when they all were close together, Andrew told them, "By the way, most winters it is very cold up here. One time the ice on the water was so thick that one could've driven a car across. It was a cinch with my bike, of course."

Hety asked, "So you have been very often up here?"

"For years I was up here at least once a month," he related, "but since they did some logging all around here with the road from Spectacle Lake improved, there're always crowds up here..."

"And you have to bring your bathing trunks," one of them remarked. He answered by holding up his thumb, which made them all laugh.

As they were rolling down the easy road toward the high tension line, not much was said until Hety stopped them again and said, "We're all from Mill Bay, Andrew, so we'll go straight on toward the cement haul road. Perhaps you want to turn left here?"

He said, "I'll go with you down to the pavement. While you most likely go along the highway, I turn left and come out at the Frayne Center. That way I never ride along the highway right to my home in Cobble Hill."

Hety called out, "But we also want to go to the Frayne Center, so we better follow you."

"In that case, let's go," he laughed, "it's a bit more rough, but much more fun."

Shaking her head, Hety couldn't help saying, "I guess you know all the roads around here, so be our

7

guide this time."

One of them heckled in fun, "Hey, we have a new leader and it's a man." It was followed by more laughter.

Before they parted later on at the Frayne Center, Andrew suggested with a question, "You think we could meet somewhere during the evening, when we're not rushed on as today to have a chat in peace and quiet?"

"I was thinking the very same," Honey said, "and wouldn't mind to ... philosophize with this man." That comment created more laughter.

Then Mira, the more quiet one of them, suggested, "I'm free tonight, we could come to my place. We all work during the day except Honey."

"Yes, let's," Hety agreed, "is seven too early?"

With a scribbled down address on a piece of paper, Andrew was the first to depart by saying with his old grin, "I really look forward to our meeting. See you then."

Looking back a bit later, he saw them still there, all smiling and chatting, no doubt about him.

* * *

Over a sandwich supper at home, Andrew wondered what would become of his new relationship with the five ladies, five nice ladies, he liked them all. But as so often when he met a woman to his liking, with very positive vibrations, she was much younger. And his experience was so far, that women always preferred younger men than themselves, men easier to control it seemed.

Later on, his thoughts were shifted to the news on TV. Then he must've dozed off because when he blinked at his watch, it already was twenty minutes to seven, high time to get going, if he wanted to find the house in time.

It was a two-story building, facing the sea of Mill Bay and the Saanich Peninsula beyond it. Three cars were parked in front of it, so they must've arrived already.

The balcony door on the second floor opened and Honey called down, "We're all up here, so just come on in and climb the stairs," she waved an inviting hand.

Entering a large room, he noticed a fireplace and it was crackling. "Hi everybody," he headed for a seat they had pointed out to him. While sitting down, he said, "I like the wood heat, it's so inviting..." Then, "I also noticed, that is my nostrils did, that there is nothing artificial in the air," and his smirky grin expressed pleasure.

Angela beside him said, "You have a fine nose, none of us use perfume when we're together."

Andrew explained, "Since I have become a vegetarian, my smelling organ has become very sensitive. First I was embarrassed at times what my nose could detect. Today I'm used to it."

Honey said, "We all will have herb tea."

"Sounds good to me," Andrew agreed.

Then Hety suggested, "Will you be so kind and tell us about your spiritual exploits, if I may call it that? I have the feeling that you know a lot."

Andrew laughed, "You give me too much credit... Often I wind up giving the wrong impression..." Then, "I've read a lot and still do. Today I've come to the conclusion that our physical universe, in which

9

we live and what we see with our eyes, is only a fraction of our whole being. The thing is, of course, to tap the other part of us, which is the spiritual part. Our intuition, that is to listen to our intuition, is a good beginning. And what is the intuition? It is soul in us. And what is soul? It is a spark of God in us. Soul is of the very same material or essence as that of God. But the most wonderful thing is, to me anyway, that soul has also the very same potential as God. This potential is latent in most of us, but one can learn to bring it out. The saints of old had it, some psychics like Edgar Cayce became famous with their abilities."

After a short while, he continued, "We shall have to learn about reincarnation, that we have lived many times before as soul. Soul reincarnates from body to body... Soul is eternal!" He said that with a very strong voice. "Much of our attention should go to our dreams and it is a good idea to have a dream journal on the night table to record them. Individually we all have a different code to unscramble their meaning which often enough is not straightforward, so to say. Our dreams at times also give us a journey into our past lifetimes. There're dream masters on the other side who will assist us in this endeavor if it is important to our spiritual growth. In any case, I happen to know some of my former lifetimes."

Then, a moment later, "All of us, as we sit here together, have been together before, as souls we know and some old recognition is there. How often do we see somebody and wham! ... we know that person! Perhaps an old love, a brother, sister, mother or father, the old love comes through and our hearts are pounding."

Honey burst out: "Boy oh boy, you're so right! You seem to know so much more than we do. Isn't there something we can read?" They all fell in with the same desire to learn more about the subject.

He replied, "It took me many years to pick up something here and something there. Some flying saucer books were of a big value. We had a group here in Duncan with our own magazine even. But that was many years back and some misconceptions also made their way into our belief. Today most of it is overhauled to a certain degree, so I will not speak about it. If I would give you the many books I've read, probably over a hundred, it just might confuse you, besides I gave most of them to the library. There is one good book, and I will lend it to you. It's called, *Journey of Souls*, by Doctor Michael Newton. It will give you a very good idea on the subject of soul, why are we here and go from body to body to learn the many lessons."

While tea was sipped, Hety asked, "Why do you think we all had been together before? I mean..."

Andrew explained, "It's well known that old acquaintances come together again and Spirit makes sure of that because old karma has to be resolved. The Law of Cause and Effect is very exact and minute," he emphasized the last sentence. "As long as old debts have to be straightened out, the Law of Karma will take care of it, one way or another, even over the period of several lifetimes. In his time Buddha spoke about it already, and ... Perhaps I should stop here. You read the book and we shall go from there on. We will meet many more times.

11

Besides," he grinned, "I don't intend to die soon, so there'll be plenty of time." That remark made them all laugh.

Then Hety asked, "Mind telling us your age?"

He laughed, "Aha, here comes the 64 dollar question, which so often stopped any further relationship, speaking out of experience... Well, with you five it might be all right. I'm 59, or should I say, I was 59 in July."

"So you're a Cancer," Honey said immediately. He just nodded and added a moment later, "I'm also a numerologist. Astrology doesn't mean much to me. Analyzing names and birthdays gives a more accurate picture of a person."

However, that admission had all the ladies talking at once. Now they wanted him to analyze their birthdays and names.

Holding up his hands in defense and laughing, he explained, "If I want to do it properly just for one of you, it would take hours. When I was deeply into this, I had to type several pages to get every minute thing down. I should've kept my mouth shut. But by your first names I know a bit about you already," he gave his smirky grin.

Hety finally commented. "It is very clear to me that some invisible force was behind our... link-up... And you had to be that old... Well, I'm only kidding." Andrew thought, 'I wonder whether she believes that?'

Then, Honey waving a finger at her, said, "Speak for yourself, Hety. I don't mind him and his age at all." That really had them all laughing and it also made Andrew realize that he had to be careful...

Until now they had been good friends. If he should get involved with one of them, it might just change the picture drastically.

It was almost eleven o'clock when they finally parted with a lot of laughs and happiness in their hearts.

* * *

Chapter 2

Surprising Disclosures

On Monday Honey called Andrew at ten in the morning and she said, "This is the girl who doesn't mind an older guy. Mind if we meet?"

Andrew replied, "Aha, you must be Honey ... I'm just preparing my lunch and in about an hour I'm at your service, madam. However, I hate to miss my daily hike, so, if you're willing to tag along, we can have a 'sniff' at each other for two or three hours."

"Couldn't you come to my place?" she asked. "Do we have to walk to talk to each other?"

He explained, "I'm used to my daily exercises on foot or with the bike, that's the best way to keep in shape. What's wrong with walking and talking, unless..."

She interrupted him with, "Then I will have to bring my lunch. Can't you eat a bit later with me together?"

"Look, Honey," he told her matter-of-factly, "I have my breakfast at four or five, so lunch for me at eleven is just right."

She didn't sound very enthused about it when she said, "Ok, Ok, I'll bring my lunch. Are you going to pick me up at my place?"

"Sounds good," he agreed, "give me your address please." So she explained where to find her house.

While preparing his soup, he thought, 'I wonder what she wants to talk about? Hopefully she doesn't think that I'm an easy catch or what. Maybe she's hard up for a man. Well, ha, ha, not this old guy. If she doesn't work, maybe she's very well off ... We'll see.' Then he thought, 'Honey, what a name, not easy to live with. I wonder whether it's her real name? At times, women adopt nicknames.'

He came to another two-story house and she had him come in first, probably to show him around, for reasons he didn't know yet. She greeted him with the words, "You sure are early... We could be very comfortable in here, but I can see on your face that you have your mind on nature."

Inhaling deeply, he replied, "It's not so much nature, although I love that part too, but to keep myself in good physical shape. And you can't beat walking, unless you're still able to jog, which I gave up last year, after I read that walking does almost the same. Look, Honey, you're still young and beautiful and probably go to bed every night feeling fresh and 'on top of the world'. I have to work at it." Then, "All right, are we going?"

She looked at him as if to say, don't rush me. After all, I'm a tender female. His grin had her pick up a bag though, which she swung over her back, letting him know that she was not very pleased. They left the house, heading for his car. With an inviting gesture, he opened the door for her and swung it closed. Behind the wheel he asked, "Any particular wish to where we should go?"

She answered, "You seem to know all the roads, so you make the choice."

While driving along the Mill Bay-Shawnigan Lake road, she occasionally glanced at him, at his lighthearted_face and thought, 'I wonder why he looks so happy? Well, I better cheer up. No reason to be gloomy, just because he didn't stay at my place. We might've a good time and we can talk in the open too... I don't know why I wanted him to stay inside with me.'

He parked at the entrance of the Cobble Hill quarry. After they had left the car, she asked surprised, "Where does this go? I thought we're going into the woods..."

"We will, Honey, we will," and he waved to follow him with a smirky grin, as he opened the unlocked gate. They might've walked a couple of hundred yards in silence, when he pointed to a hardly-visible house, hidden behind bushes and high trees, and explained, "At this point I usually give off a certain whistle, and my doggy friend would come running from there to join me. For over ten years we two were hiking companions, but last year they had to put her to sleep because of old age. She hardly could walk anymore." He had said that with an unusual seriousness, she also noticed his blinking eyes. "Tracy and I were very close ... we had a deep love for each other."

Seeing his pained face, Honey uttered, "I'm very sorry, Andrew..."

"It's all right," he answered, "when I pass by here at times, it still stirs my emotions." He wiped his eyes and grinned again, as if it was nothing.

After a half a kilometer or so, they turned left onto a gravel road, winding up a hill slowly. She asked, "Why can't you have your own dog? I mean…"

His explanation surprised her, "Living on your own makes a poor relationship between dog and human being I think. In my case, what does one do when driving into town, going on long holidays, riding his bike and what have you? I can see and hear it all the time where I live. Dogs bark and bark while the owner is not at home, or they put it into a kennel, where it is not very happy, as everybody can imagine. And to begin with, why do we have a dog? For our own pleasure only? What about the dog? It can't speak and express itself. Doesn't a love relationship go both ways?"

A moment later, he added, "I sleep every night with an open window and can hear the same dog bark every night, all night long. Haven't those people any feelings toward their so-called dog friend? If it wasn't some distance away, I would go there and give those people a 'piece' of my mind."

After arriving on top of the hill, Honey was surprised at the sight. He explained, "As you can see, the old quarry is now filled with water and a company is raising fish in there. During the summer, some children come for a swim, often accompanied by their parents. The water-filled fields beyond are used to plant potatoes when it's dry enough again. The whole area around the quarry is already divided into hundreds of lots. In ten or twenty years, we might see many houses being built down there. They already drilled the wells for the water supply."

Honey had taken a seat on a large rock and began to eat her lunch to his "Bon appétit."

With a foot raised on a pile of gravel, Andrew ventured to say, "With the present world situation, where fanatics blow themselves up to kill others with different convictions and where workers have lost their jobs because a recession or depression kind of is upon us, a lot of rethinking has to be done. Maybe the houses down there will never be built." Then, "You know, I always wondered how the next world war would begin? One never knows, this could be it."

Looking at Honey, he noticed that she had stopped eating... With a grave face she uttered, "I'm not hungry anymore..."

"Oh, blast it!" he called out, "it's my fault! Sometimes I need a clamp on my mouth." Then, "Come on, Honey, you can eat a bit more..." But she shook her head. He tried to coax her with the words, "Think about Spirit, the way It's guiding and protecting us..." But it was no use. She fed the rest of the sandwich to a couple of crows, who were patiently waiting for a morsel.

Suddenly then she stood up, took his hand, and said to his surprise, "I like you a lot, Andrew. You have a way of explaining and it makes sense."

Thinking for a moment, he looked at her, then asked, "Is Honey your real name?"

She nodded, "Yes, why?"

He wondered whether he should tell her that by numerology her name was difficult to live with. She grabbed his hand again and said, "Aha, you analyzed it and... Come on, you must tell me, Andrew," she called out.

Shrugging his shoulders with a smile, he said, "We actually didn't want to do it, but ... well ... I had to open my mouth again." Patting her hand, he asked, "Did you ever wonder that you cannot pull yourself away from the mistakes you've made? They stick to you like burdock and you ask yourself, 'Why am I doing it again and again?' It never seems to end."

Looking at him very intensely, she called out, "Yes, yes, yes, that's my life and it has followed me since I was a young girl."

Then she heard him ask, "What's your birthday, Honey?"

"January the 19th, 1970," she replied.

Thinking for a while and shaking his head, he finally said, "I'm not surprised, my dearest one. It must be like a heavy weight on your system ... your activities ... you should be born a man."

Under loud crying and hanging onto him, she burst out, "On top of it, I'm also a bisexual and can't have a normal relationship with a man." With his arms around her, she held both of her hands in front of her face, shaking with sobs.

'What now?' Andrew asked himself. 'I can't push her away, after all, I started it. She needs my comfort now, that's for sure,' He was thinking hard, 'Should I help this woman? It might get out of hand... Why has Spirit put us together? It might be a hold-over from a past life!' Out loud he said, "Please, Honey, you must stop crying. Perhaps I can help you."

Out of his arms and calmed down considerably, she heard him suggest, "Let's create a fresher atmos-

19

phere and walk in the woods." He led her onto a narrow trail, where they had to walk behind each other.

When they could walk abreast again, he asked, "I guess you've considered an operation?"

"They wanted to make a man out of me," she almost shouted, "I'm a woman ... Just look at my breasts ... No way! I think and feel like a woman."

He had taken her hand, and rather quietly suggested, "By leaving the 'e' out of your name, it would become balanced and help you a lot!" he emphasized. "It takes a long time, of course, although some people experienced rather quick results. By your birthdate, it would be easier to be a man, it's perfect for a pioneer of old. However, we must remember that the birthdate qualities are put upon us to learn certain lessons, things we did not learn in a past lifetime. Why are you born in this life as a bisexual? The question should be rather, what did you do in former lifetimes to cause that? Perhaps it will be shown to you in a dream... That's why it's so important to keep a dream journal. There are beings in the other worlds who will help you to understand, but you must recognize it first and then take the initiative and give it an effort."

She had hooked into his arm, and so they walked for a long time until Andrew spoke again, "The book by Doctor Newton will put a lot of light on this, and it also might give you an idea perhaps why we two are together now, certainly not to live together, if that had been on your mind. Perhaps I might be able to help you because I'm very knowledgeable about many things you never even heard of. And to come to your plight as a bisexual... I have a lot of books by world famous physicians, and in there you might find a way to have a good relationship with a man. At one time, those books didn't do me much good, but they might be of help to you."

A bit later, he came back to the same subject, "Many years ago I had a nice partner and thought I had it made. Then at 25 I had the idea that sex was the spice of a good relationship, but my marriage went broke and why? Because she wanted love, not the physical love, but the love of heart and soul, of which I didn't have a clue. Here I was with all the books about sex, but as a woman she wanted a different kind of love. On my own then again, I was introduced to Spirit, that our heart and soul are the main ingredients of that love. After all those years, today I'm able to give this love and will feel it when returned, particularly from a little child or a dog even."

After a while, he said once more, "As devastated as I was at the break-up of my marriage then, today I have learned to live by the positive virtues with the main ingredient of love. Perhaps some day I'll find a partner again I'm able to share this love with, that is, the whole spectrum of love. However, I'm also a realist ... The age of mine is not in my favor."

For a long time they walked without words between them. Impulsively then — while her mind and heart also had been on the crossroad of realization — she had taken his hand and asked, "Mind if I hold you like that? It gives me comfort."

He nodded and replied, "It also gives me comfort, Honey, for I'm very physical and a sensitive person and feel your positive vibrations."

Much later then, he suggested, "Let's not do this

in front of the others because they might draw the wrong conclusion. Most of the many things we've spoken of today are between us two. I might have something similar with the other girls also, although not individually. You five are good friends, and this old guy will not come in between you, but rather have a good friendship with all of you." Then, "Do any of the others know of our meeting?"

"I told Hety," she replied, "and she also knows that I'm bisexual. She has comforted me here and there when I was emotionally on my knees, so to speak. She's a very strong woman."

As they were driving through Mill Bay much later, Honey suddenly said, "I just see our bookstore there, I wouldn't mind to get that book. Let's go and see whether they've got it?"

Surprised, the lady in the store said, "You're the third person buying it today. The others phoned in to hold it for them."

Andrew laughed and suggested in fun, "Some strange force seems to be at work..."

"You've got the last one of it," the lady said, "we better order more of them."

In front of her house and still inside the car, Honey took his hands and pleaded, "Do come in for a tea, please, and write that down with my name and birthdate. I want to know more about it. Perhaps it will help me."

Seated in her living room, he explained, "But do remember, Honey, as you get more and more involved with Spirit, your dreams, reincarnation, the Law of Karma and how it's all linked together and how it works, this numerology concept moves into the background, including our relationship. For now I will not cram your mind more. Eventually, things will come to you, if you keep your mind open enough. You yourself must want it though, and not because I say it and told you."

She couldn't help saying, "Hopefully, we two will see each other more often. I've become very fond of you," and she put her arm around him again.

He laughed and poked her nose, "Let's not make it too much of a habit. No doubt you will come up with questions and we can discuss them." Then, in a funny jest, "I'm probably still around for another fifty years, ha ha, and going by today, when I picked you up in the morning and now, you will have become a saint, I'm sure of it."

With a genuine laugh, probably the first in some years, and a free and happy heart, Honey sent him off with a wave of her hand. After she had closed the house door, she thought, 'And to think that ... that ... I was almost angry with him... How stupid of me... He has so much to offer like no other person I ever met before. And now I shall read the book, *Journey of Souls*. What will it reveal to me?'

* * *

On the very same day at seven that evening, Hety phoned Andrew and said, "Mind if we have a chat, away from the others?"

"All right," he simply said, "I could come right now."

She asked, "Did you see Honey?"

"I did," he answered with a grin to himself. Then she gave him her address.

While driving toward her place, Andrew thought,

'Let's see what she has on her mind. Perhaps she is concerned about Honey and wants to find out what we did and talked about?'

The house was rather small, but it stood on a large lot with a very well-maintained garden. 'It's a picture for a postcard,' he thought. There was no garage and he didn't see a car. While walking along the stone lane toward the house door, he thought. 'What a surprise ... Perhaps she doesn't drive.'

The door was a bit open and he heard her voice, "Come on in, Andrew. I've my hands wet here in the kitchen sink. I didn't think you were that fast." Meeting him, while wiping her hands, she suggested, "Sit down on this chair, later on we can go into the living room. I want to keep an eye on the preserves in that big pot on the stove. So, what have you two been up to, if I may ask?"

He grinned, "You want to have it very blunt and straightforward, or no answer at all?"

She looked at him, knowing very well how he meant it, then said, while patting his hand over the table, "I'm very concerned about Honey... But perhaps you're way ahead of me and were a big help to her..."

He answered, "I have the impression, and I have an eye for this kind of 'stuff', that you might be the most matured of the girls, or should I have said ladies. Being much older doesn't give me the right to belittle you."

She got up and waved to him to follow her to sit on a wooden bench together. Then she said, "You don't know how comfortable I am with you because you portray so much trust and knowledge. Well, I'm the oldest at 39 and the only one not divorced yet. My husband didn't abuse me physically, but he got to me in other ways, like no divorce, for instance."

Looking at him and inhaling deeply, she said, "I miss a mate very much. Not him, but a man I can love. It's in my nature I guess, that I want the physical feel of a man. I know without your telling me that you never would get involved with Honey, besides ... I guess, she's told you?" he nodded.

Then after several coaxing tries from within, she finally said, "You're much more mature than I am, your whole behavior, your handshake and your eyes told me. What would I give to have a man like you because with you a woman will feel comfortable... She will feel like a woman because you'll let her." She continued with a fleeting breath, "So, here it goes, this woman wants you... If only once a week, Andrew. I can love you with all my heart and soul and I know I would get the very same from you."

Andrew could feel and hear her heart pounding... So he took one of her hands to his lips and kissed it, while his eyes looked into hers. "I could come up with all kinds of reasons," he began, "pertaining to the relationship toward the other girls. I could raise the question of ethics, of responsibilities... Guilt, sin and the like, have no part in my life anymore. Some people would think I'm weak, but my physical nature is too strong for that. So Hety, how can I say no to such a genuine wish and desire where lust is non-existent. This man also wants to give and receive love ... very much though, it's deeply anchored in my nature."

After they had parted from their embrace and a deep kiss, he suggested, "It would be best to come to my place and I leave the days to you. I could pick you up."

"I have a car in my neighbor's garage," she explained with a fleeing voice. "Will Wednesday at eight be all right?" Putting her arms around him again, she whispered, "Oh Andrew, you don't know the relief it gives me. My deep desire to love and to be loved was not natural anymore. It will make me a better woman and human being again."

Before he left the house, she squeezed him once more, "Oh Andrew, you... Spirit has put us together. I'm sure of it."

Her eyes followed him all the way to the car. Before entering, he turned around with a smile and waved. During the drive home he thought, 'By God, I will love this woman with all my heart and soul...'

* * *

Two days later, Honey phoned Andrew again and asked, "Can I join you for another hike? I'll have an early lunch, so I'll be ready."

"You sound so cheerful," he bantered with her, "but I wanted to go swimming first and then walk near Duncan."

"I've a bathing suit... Can I come?" she asked at once.

He laughed, "It must be important..."

"It is, it is," she interrupted him. "I've read the whole book and have many questions."

"I might as well give in ... or ..."

"I won't be a pest, I promise," she said with excitement. "Can I come to your place? I want to see how you live."

"Do I have any choice?" he laughed.

26

After he had hung up, he thought, 'Obviously a big change has penetrated her. Oh, to be so young again, and so enthusiastic with the knowledge of today. I wonder what else Spirit has in store for me? Having connected me with the five girls ... or women...' "No, they're ladies, Andrew," he said out loud to himself.

Of course, Hony — now spelled without the 'e' — was full of all the news she had up her 'sleeve', so to speak. "First I want to walk through your house, and don't say anything." So, he followed her, grinning and smiling to himself. Inside his bedroom she commented, "So you make your bed every day." A bit later, she followed it with the words, "Although it won't be me, you need a woman. I've an eye for that." He just nodded with pleasure. There definitely was a new being in this girl, he observed.

After they had made the rounds, she commented, "Now I know a bit more about you, Andrew. OK, I'm ready to go, and we can take my car, if it's all right with you?" He just nodded.

While driving toward Duncan, she couldn't help saying, "You are so quiet, but your smile tells me that everything is OK. Mind telling me?"

He replied, "You don't know the pleasure you're giving me with your new state of mind, your new state of everything. I do absorb it with a deep feeling. What are words, Hony?" He patted one of her hands on the steering wheel.

Suddenly, she asked rather shyly, "You love me, Andrew?"

"Yes, I do, Hony."

After they had parked the car at the Cowichan

Community Centre, she took one of his hands and said, "I know the meaning of our love. It is the love of Soul." He just nodded.

Before they left the car, she leaned over to kiss him on the cheek. Then she suggested, "Let's go for a swim."

He was sitting in the hot pool, where she discovered him. "Boy, this is hot, Andrew." Slowly she made her way into the water to sit beside him. Then she whispered, "Why are those men looking at us?"

He whispered back, "They're my old swimming companions and now they wonder that I have caught myself a young girl like you, ha ha."

"Ha ha," she laughed back, "let them, maybe they're jealous." They both burst out laughing. "Come on," she coaxed him, "Let's go swimming," and he followed her into the big pool, where she did some more laughing.

While swimming side by side, he couldn't help reminding her, "Only a few days ago I distinctly remember a certain young girl, vying for an older man... That goes the other way too, Hony. What I mean is, men have their eyes on young girls, perhaps even more so."

At once she admitted, "You're right, of course, I shall not belittle them again."

After having gone leisurely four times the length of the pool behind each other, Andrew suggested, "I'm ready for our hike. I've had enough." She nodded and they left for their dressing rooms.

It had begun to rain when they met at the car and he said with some disappointment, "In my car I would've had an umbrella..."

However, his young companion was not to be held back and she suggested, "We'll buy one, a big one for both of us." He said nothing, just grinned at her initiative and thought, 'I'll just let her. How can I sour her enthusiasm?'

Coming out of the mall again, the rain had stopped, but she said with satisfaction, "I needed one anyway."

As Andrew was directing her down a road, she called out with much surprise, "I've never been down here before."

"Well," he left the car and said, "the old railroad to Cowichan Lake used to go along here. It was before your time. I remember standing on that bridge and following it under me... Today we hikers, bike riders and horse people use it. Hey, let's not forget the umbrella..."

She laughed, "I almost forgot. Let's not get wet, the sky does not look inviting."

On the way, with her hooked into his arm, he said, "I'd like to come back once more to the affair of belittling. A better word is ridicule perhaps. It's very common today, but I try to stay away from it because it's a negative passion."

She squeezed his arm and said, "I will listen to your wise words, Andrew."

Under the newly-built cement bridge and seeing the rushing creek water, she aired her hope, "I trust we don't have to go across it..."

He replied, "We don't <u>have</u> to do anything, Hony, unless we really want to."

Some time later, and referring to the book, *Journey of Souls*, she asked, "You think we knew each other as souls?"

A moment later, he ventured to say, "I don't know that, but we have been together in past lifetimes. You five girls probably knew each other as souls and talked it over, what lesson had to be learned and what body to enter in this lifetime. Being together again today might indicate that you knew each other as souls. As long as some karma is between you, and us two also, we can be sure that the opportunity is given to dissolve it. All this is so intricate, that our minds at the present cannot conceive it. So we make the best out of our immediate environment, what we can see now!"

After a long walk in silence, Hony brought up the subject of soul guides, as mentioned in the book. He explained, "I think they're the lords of karma, as I understand it today. They're minor deities, working for the lord of the lower worlds. They know the karma of every soul and what to do next to work it out. It's a vast subject, too vast for us to delve into. We have to remember that Spirit, the current coming from the Supreme Godhead, is behind everything. I just mentioned the book by Doctor Newton for you to understand the workings 'behind the scenes', so to speak. The most valuable thing we can pluck out of it is to observe our passions and virtues for spiritual growth. However, on our own and without any help, we might find it very difficult. So, we have to find a guide, a master who will help us in this endeavor, somebody who went through all this many years or even lifetimes ago, somebody who is God-Realized and is the direct agent of God."

Then he laughed out loud, "And now let's attend

to some physical matter and try to get across the creek... There're some trees fallen across it, but they would be too slippery right now. There also is a fallen down bridge. Let's see whether we still can use it."

They had to walk single file, and when they came to the bridge, leaning badly over to one side, he asked, "You think you can balance over it?"

She grabbed his arm and said, "If you can, so can I."

"Use your umbrella to steady yourself," he advised.

It was easy enough though because somebody had nailed a plank across, easy to walk on without slipping. He explained, "Many years back, there used to be a house down here, as you can see by the electrical wires still overhead."

With about half of their hike behind them, Hony asked, "Who are those high masters you mentioned? I don't understand that."

He thought for a moment, then tried to explain, "These beings are God-Realized with vast God powers. What we as souls are trying today, they already managed to do many years back, with discipline, love and going by the virtues, while ignoring the negative passions, like anger, vanity, lust and greed, to give some examples. Out of Greek history we know the famous mathematician Pythagoras. They say that he had vast God powers and knowledge. And there also was the famous Plato, who spoke the well-known sentence, 'Know thyself!' which means, of course, soul within us. Not many understood the meaning of it then and how many understand it today...? The meaning of it is that soul is eternal, it never dies. Those two were masters of a very high standing, they were agents of the Supreme Deity. Today, I've come to the conclusion that we need one of those greats to get anywhere spiritually. I have no illusions about that, and they will make themselves known to the ready person."

A bit later, he added, "In the meantime, let's attend to our physical environment and needs. Living on a cloud of hope and prayer will get us nowhere, or even make fanatics out of us, like those terrorists, believing they wind up on the right side of their god with their hatred and destructive actions. It is a case of the blind brainwashing the blind..."

Almost back at the car, she asked, "Are you seeing Hety?"

He began to laugh, "Right now I'm seeing you, Hony."

At once she replied, "I know I shouldn't have asked."

He suggested with a grin at her, "Let's keep our private lives apart. We're not revealing everything to each other."

Halfway back to Cobble Hill, Andrew asked, "Would you like to meet my two lady friends at Valleyview? In the health food store there they're serving the most delicious drink, called a smoothy."

"Aha," she laughed, "some more women come into the picture."

Laughing back, he said, "Men are so terribly uninteresting and outright dull... Well," he grinned, "not all of them."

After the introductions had been made inside the store, Andrew explained, "On this smoothy one can live all day long without any other food. It's nutritionally complete."

Hony said at once, "There is something else you have to teach me."

After they had parked at Andrew's house, she asked haltingly, "You think I can join you more often? I can use those walks also because I'm getting flabby..."

He agreed, "So often I was thinking of a hiking companion, somebody I can share nature with and have a conversation here and there, reminding me that I'm still a human being."

Then she explained, "By the way, next weekend there will be a Christmas party at my place and you're invited. We five adopted a woman with her three children, and she's going to be there also. Her husband is very old and not mentally responsible anymore. Tomorrow I still can join you, but from then on I'm too busy for the rest of the week."

He asked, "If you need help... You know where I live." Then he said, "Boy oh boy, Christmas already. I almost had forgotten it. Well, not really, the kids in my neighborhood are big reminders."

Before she drove off, he suggested, "Please make sure that I'm home and give me a ring first, every time you intend to come."

Outside the car and with him leaning down, she suddenly pulled him into the open window and gave him a kiss, then said smilingly, "You deserved that, Andrew." And off she drove.

Following her car, he thought with an inner smile, 'I'll be safe with her. That soul has become alive and liberated.'

Entering his house and inhaling deeply, he thought, 'She will bring joy to our hikes. It'll be good to see her again tomorrow.'

Next day and driving toward Glenora, Hony was telling Andrew, "I've never been down this way."

He replied, "I used to have a good friend down here, but he died four years ago. On my visits I often explored the forests around here on my own, particularly along the Cowichan River area. In the meantime they have made a park out of it and it's a beauty with plant life no place else to be found. My most favorite hikes are around Glenora. I shall introduce you to all that in the year of 2002." She gave him a happy smile.

Sitting on a fallen tree halfway across the river were several bald eagles, waiting patiently to catch a fish. They were floating down the rushing water, now dead from the earlier salmon run. At times the water was so high that it flashed over their trail, but they wore their water-tight boots. Hony said with joy in her voice, "Oh Andrew, without you I never would've experienced this." Then, "Next time we'll go here with the other girls too."

Much later and walking along the newly-opened Trans-Canada Trail back to their car, she brought up the subject of the books on sex he had mentioned on their first hike together. Whether they might be of help to her, having a better physical relationship with a man as a bisexual.

Thinking for a while about her request, he seriously shook his head and suggested, "Please Hony, don't fill yourself with what's written in those books at this time, although they might be of help to you someday. You're so happy at the moment because so many new concepts have made their way into your consciousness. Digest the newly-won knowledge and be happy for a while. You're still young and this old guy will not run away and I'll be around for some time to come. I understand you, of course, having been disappointed by a man and divorced now. When the time is more ripe in early 2002, approach me again, OK?"

*   *   *

When Hety entered Andrew's house a few hours later at eight, the very first thing she said with a fleeting voice, "I feel awfully guilty, Andrew ... that I approached you like that..."

He put an arm around her and directed her to the sofa in the living room, where she sat down beside him. With a serious voice he said, "The tools of the negative are guilt, sin and what have you. They're used by people who want to have a hold on us. How many people are 'living in sin', as our society calls it, and it makes them feel guilty about it. By some religions we're born in sin and are all sinners... It puts a terrible guilt feeling on the listeners. Be free from all that, Hety."

Then he said rather determined, "God has made us all free! It is not for somebody to take that freedom away from us. Why should you feel guilty? Because you're a woman? You had the courage to approach me with love... What can be more noble than a woman's courage? What if this rather old guy would've made the first move? You see, my dearest one..." He held her hand to his heart, "A woman's honest desire and love will not tolerate guilt, or sin, or any of the other negative passions."

Then he suggested, "Come, let's walk around the

block in the fresh air," he pulled her up. "So often words are useless, so our hearts and souls will do the communicating."

Some time later and still in each other's arms, Hety whispered, "You think we could see each other perhaps more than once a week?"

"How can we put a time-limit on love, on our love?" he replied.

* * *

Chapter 3

The Christmas Party

Hony phoned Andrew early and said, "You wanted to help... We'll be here at my place at about one, or you want to go on your hike first?"

"Oh girl," he called out, "did I give you the impression that I absolutely have to go on my hike every day?" Then, "But I don't mind coming a bit earlier to have a look at <u>your</u> place, and walk from room to room, ha ha."

"Well," she began hesitantly, "we're actually already here at twelve and have a pizza lunch, but..."

He laughed and said, "If it's a vegetarian pizza, I wouldn't mind joining you guys."

"You would, hey?" she bantered with him, "we'll make sure it's vegetarian. How about you come at ten already? That should give you ample time to inspect my place."

He called out, "I agree, Hony. I hardly can wait."

'Oh that man,' Hony thought, after he had hung up, 'to find a man like him... What would I give?' Happily she awaited his coming.

At shortly after ten, Andrew drove up at Hony's place to surprise her with a big bunch of beautiful flowers. "For me?" she greeted him at the door.

"It's for all of you, Hony, to cheer up the occasion."

"Oh," she sounded disappointed.

He held onto her and said, "Look at me, girl, let's not go beyond our present state of happiness..."

She replied, "It's just that you're so nice and where will I ever find a man like you?"

He led her into the kitchen and said with relaxed and soothing words, "You will, Hony, your age is in your favor."

While arranging the bouquet of flowers in a water-filled vase, she commented, "They're beautiful... Where did you get them so early?"

"I bought them yesterday," he grinned, "not knowing exactly what for. But today they come to good use."

A bit later he asked, "Will they all be here?"

She nodded and said, "Getta might go to her sister in Vancouver. She doesn't know yet. Angela with the big car will pick them all up. I don't think that any of them will work on this Saturday."

Then he suggested, "OK, would you be so kind and lead me around your house...?"

She answered with a smile, "It's as big as yours..." At her upstairs bedroom, she commented, "As you can see, I also make my bed every day and I also have a feather down cover..."

He thought, 'I better not say anything... Obviously, she is terribly lonely.' A bit later, he complimented her with the words, "Your house is spotless, Hony. I have to hire a woman to do my place. I honestly don't know why I ever bought a big place like that, most of the rooms are never used. My cleaning lady only charges me 15 dollars and her eyes are telling me what she thinks, namely that I'm crazy to hire her for the little work. But … I'm not cut out to do any housework, it's not in my stars, ha ha."

Hony took him by the arm and said, "I could say something about that, Andrew, but I won't…" They grinned at each other, and it said the rest.

As the four marched up the outdoor stairs later on, he opened the door quickly and called out: "Surprise!"

In front, Mira hastened out the question, "What are you doing here?"

"You'll get three guesses," he smiled.

However, Hony couldn't help but saying, "He's Santa Claus, ha ha ha. We need a male helper, don't we?" All laughed and entered the house, taking their coats off.

Then Hony explained, "We two have been hiking for the last two days, and when Andrew offered his help, I phoned him this morning. He was here faster than the wind, ha ha."

"His love for us all is very obvious," Mira couldn't resist saying.

So he quickly took her into his arms and asked, "How did you know?" It gave all the girls a satisfying feeling.

Andrew suggested then with his smirky grin, "For this special occasion I would like to put my arms around each of you and give you a squeeze. You see this old bachelor was all by himself for many years around Christmas, and now I have the pleasure to be with five beautiful girls, ladies, movie stars… To me you are all of them. Here we go…" After the last embrace, he couldn't help saying, "You sure made my day, girls."

At that moment, the pizza delivery man was at the door and Hony said, "Today it'll be vegetarian because our man," she pointed to him, "is a vegetarian."

With the pizza still hot, they all sat down in the kitchen to eat. So much talking and laughing was going on, that Andrew finally said with his old grin, "One thing I've never learned during my 59 years, is to eat and talk… But, please, do continue. I don't eat with my ears." Which caused a hearty laugh by them all.

Then Angela said with a grin, "I believe we got ourselves the right man, he lets us talk." That comment really made them laugh.

Later, with the Christmas tree brought in, they discovered that it was too tall. "What now?" Hety called out.

"I've all kind of tools in the trunk of my car, including a saw," Andrew soothed their concern, "I'll be back in a minute."

With a foot cut off, the tree still didn't fit into the three-legged holder. So Andrew worked with his machete on the wood and had it fit in five minutes. He commented, "Look at the tree trunks today. Many people have the same trouble to make it fit."

Then the boxes with the many decorations were brought in and during the late afternoon, a beautiful Christmas tree stood in their midst.

"You know something," Hony said with satisfaction, "with everything done already, with the exceptions of the gifts tomorrow, we actually could go on a hike before the reception... What do you say guys?" Then, "We could go to Glenora where Andrew and I went yesterday... It's really wild there, I tell you. Well...?"

"You're so quiet," Hety looked at him...

He raised his shoulders and said, "I'm free all day, in fact, I'm free all Christmas. If it wasn't for you ladies, I probably would be sitting at home all by myself... Well, what do you ladies want? I'm just tagging along, whatever you decide."

"We always vote, you guys," Getta said. They decided to go. Before they parted, Andrew had his say once more, "Tomorrow is Sunday, the day before Christmas Eve. I would like to contribute a bit more than just my physical labor. Mind if I take you all out for a lunch before the hike?"

"Oh Andrew," Mira said at once, "you don't have to do that..."

Suddenly everybody wanted to say something at once, so he just sat down on the sofa and listened with a smile. When they had quieted down, he said with his smirky grin, "I could tell you that I'm rather well off with more than enough of a monthly income, that I easily can afford five ladies with an enormous appetite. I also could tell you that it would be so nice if we six souls simply could love each other and quietly fill our bodies with some nutritious food, so that there won't be any breakdown on this rather arduous hike along the Cowichan River in Glenora... I also could tell you..."

Hety sat down beside him and said with some

seriousness in her voice, "We'll be honored to accept your invitation." Then she looked with some pretended seriousness at the other girls and called out, "Shut up, you guys, of course we'll go."

Getting up suddenly and pointing a thumb to himself, he said, "My supper has to be prepared..." He left the house with a grin and was gone.

Hety said then, "If he wants to give, we should not argue about it and let him. I have the feeling that he is very happy with us and probably more than likes us. On his own he might be very lonely."

Hony sat down beside her and added, "You're so right. He's a very good-hearted man. I found that out during our hikes. He has a lot to offer and I've learned a lot from him. Please don't laugh. He's made it very clear that with our age difference it would be ridiculous to be more than good friends. 'As souls we love, Hony,' he told me. And that's the very same with you guys. I'm very comfortable with Andrew. He's not what I first thought of him. With him I can relax... You know very well what most of the other men want."

Hety patted her hand and nodded with agreement and thought, 'She could be more than right... I kind of wonder, would he have approached me? Probably not as an older man. Yes, of course, it had to be me, the much younger woman.' That thought made her very happy.

* * *

It was established by phone that they all would meet at the Pioneer House, south of Duncan, one hour before noon. Andrew had reserved a table to where he guided the ladies with a "Hi everybody," and his usual smile.

With a menu placed before everyone of them, Andrew said, "Please, ladies, don't have second thoughts of what to order. You all have been the nicest Christmas present to this man I can think of. Perhaps in a small way I also can give something back to you with this lunch. So, be so kind, and don't look at the prices, but simply order, period."

Getta began with, "But..." Then she noticed Hety's stern look at her with the words not spoken out behind her held-up hand, but moved with her lips: Shut up! She had noticed it at once and understood very well."

When the ordering began, Andrew suggested, "If anybody feels like a glass of wine, please..." he made an inviting move with his hand.

Toward the end of the meal, Hety explained, "Perhaps this is a good time, Andrew, to tell you a bit about Halge and her children. We kind of adopted them on special days, like this Christmas for instance. It's more for her children, Julia, the oldest at 12, the boy Floyd at 9 and Louise at 6. You see, their father is mentally not receptive anymore. He has Jewish faith, but Halge is kind of trying to get away from it now. It's ticklish all right, where it concerns the children. But she approached Mira — they're neighbors — and so we all came into the picture a year or so ago, to help where we can. Naturally, this Christmas we invited them to our party. They're well-to-do, so she doesn't want any expensive gifts, but a joyful atmosphere with songs and laughter."

Andrew couldn't help but saying, "That is very intriguing to me... I'm very grateful that you thought of me. I will do my part."

On their way to Glenora, the ladies in their car sang a happy Christmas song and it lifted them into the right mood.

Out of their cars, Andrew asked, "Which way shall we go? Hony and I went to the river first... How about we begin with the Trans-Canada Trail and then loop back along the river?"

"You lead the way," Angela called out. Since they were able to walk in twos, he asked, "Will you be my partner, Angela, for the first stretch of the walk?" She hooked into his arm and off they were.

At times Andrew walked backward to explain something of interest, so that they didn't have to slow down or stop. At one time they asked him, "Hony spells herself now without the 'e'... What about our names?"

It took him a while to find the right answer, then he explained, "Hony's first name was outright detrimental, it hurt me when I analyzed it. I can do your names too at the first opportunity and see how balanced you are. Let me remind you that I never would favor anyone of you. And please let's not forget, our spiritual aspect of life is much more important."

More than half an hour of easy walk along the trail, Andrew pointed to their right into the high trees and bushes and asked, "Can you see the river through there? Are you all feeling like getting off this trail for a shortcut through the bushes? We might encounter some bear and cougars..." he added with his smirky grin. "But if you don't feel comfortable..."

Getta asked with concern, "You mean off this beaten path and..."

Hony called out, "He's kidding us... Bear and cougars, ha ha, and some snakes probably, ha ha."

"Come on, you guys," Hety coaxed them, "we don't have to vote for that. Lead the way, Andrew, we're going."

Although slow going, it was easy enough down a steep slope, squeezing through some dense and thorny bushes and in about thirty minutes they hit the return trail. Soon they reached a sign with an arrow: Cowichan River. The rushing water was very noisy and they had to keep their eyes on the up and down trail, often going right down to the water level. It was an arduous exercise for everyone.

Coming close to Andrew at one point, Getta asked, "Are there really bear and cougars in this forest?"

They all had come close to hear his answer, "Almost every week you read in the papers about a tranquilized cougar because it came too close to people and their houses. They're not making that up, Getta. And bear? I've encountered many, but never came close enough to take a good picture. I'm never without my camera," he patted on his pocket. "And cougars, as smart as they are, know of course that I want to take their picture, so they stay away." It took a moment to catch on, and then they all burst out laughing.

When they came to a newly-built bridge over a small creek, Andrew suggested, "This is a good spot to take a picture of us all together." With the self-timer set, he ran toward the girls, and they all put their arms around each other. It was just in time, when the flash lit up. So a half a dozen more pictures were taken, in different positions and a lot of laughs.

Finally, Andrew led them up some very old, almost

rotten wooden steps, and he explained, "Hopefully they will replace them some day and not take them out all together. Not many people know of their existence. I discovered them by accident, going, as so often, off the beaten path through the dense bush," he chuckled about his explanation.

They all began to wonder why they never had been in this wild and beautiful park in Glenora, along the Cowichan River.

Back in Mill Bay, Hony said to Andrew, "You will come to our Christmas party and meet Halge and the children, will you?"

"How can I refuse your invitation," he turned back from his car. Then he asked, "Can I bring anything, gifts or what?"

"Bring your happiness," Angela called out. They all nodded.

* * *

Walking up to Hony's house on Christmas Eve, Andrew held a bouquet of red carnations behind his back, but they had seen it through the window. Opening the door, Hony said, "You can't hide them from us. Come on in and welcome!" Holding the flowers to her nose, she couldn't help but say, "What fragrance..."

After he had taken off his jacket and entered the living room, he called out, "Merry Christmas to all of you. There is a carnation for everyone of you ladies and with them comes my love."

Then, looking at Halge, he burst out, "I know you! But... but..." Bending down and taking her hand, he said, "But from where?"

They all had stopped talking and put their atten-

46

tion on the two. Swallowing hard, he raised her hand to his lips.

Realizing finally that he was completely out of order, he apologized, "I'm awfully sorry, but I know you Halge, from where I don't remember. Please forgive me, all of you... Although my heart is still thumping, I should've controlled myself better. Do old guys ever learn?" He gave his old laugh.

Then he faced the three children to shake their hands, while saying, "Would you be so kind and introduce yourselves. I hate to get you mixed up," he explained with his old smirky grin.

The six-year-old Louise immediately raised the question, "How can you mix us up, sir? I'm only six and Julia is already twelve."

Banging his forehead, he called out, "Of course! I'm not myself today. Thanks for reminding me, Louise." And he held up his flat hand, which she slapped with a grin.

"By the way," Andrew informed them, "I'm Andrew to all of you, none of this sir stuff, please." Then he shook hands with the other two children, while they said their names.

Then he grabbed one of the lighter kitchen chairs and sat himself across from the Copperfield family. In about five minutes, he had particularly the children laughing. Then he said, "I have a beautiful workshop at home with a direct telephone line to Santa Claus, and I can build anything you can think of."

The six-year-old Louise advised him, "We're not believing in Santa Claus anymore."

"Well," Andrew replied with a wise nod, "when you become old enough, you find out that the parents are the ones who put things under the tree."

A moment later, he continued, "Hey, I've got to tell you this story which happened to me when I was about your age, Floyd. I was very much in love with a neighbor girl and I wanted to take a picture of her, but I was too shy to ask her. So I rigged up my old box camera outside in the ivy, which grew up the house wall. With a long string on the lever I thought I could take a picture of her, when she was leaving the house. But I pulled too hard in my excitement and the camera fell out of the ivy in front of her feet. So she picked it up and brought it back to me inside the house and said, "You'll never guess what just happened to me on your doorstep. This camera was dropped down on me... You think...?" And she handed the camera to me. With a shaking head she left the house. Of course, I didn't say anything, but she might've had second thoughts about the validity of Santa."

By now all the ladies, including Halge, were laughing, and Hety called out, "You're making this up, Andrew! It wasn't true, or?"

With the most honest face, he replied, "Are you trying to expose this most serious and truthful story-teller?"

That remark had particularly the children's mother laughing, and she said, "I watched the children's faces and for a moment was drawn into the story also."

"Hey, you guys," Andrew said grinning, "here is another story you want..."

"No, no," Hony called out, "that story has to wait. There're some gifts in the big cardboard box and Getta will do us the honor and take them out, while Julia will be so kind and read the names."

Floyd and Louise showed some excitement. There was a lot of ohs and laughs by the ladies. Finally, Getta pulled out the last gift and Julia read, "Andrew."

Surprised, he called out, "You must be kidding... Santa doesn't even know of my existence ... ha ha."

"This Santa does," all the girls called out. Unwrapping the small box, a little red heart with a gold chain came to light. Holding it up and looking around, he simply asked, "For me?"

While Getta put it around his neck, she said in a rather quiet tone, "We all love you Andrew."

He was swallowing hard and some tears rolled down his cheeks. Wiping them off with his handkerchief, he replied, "It looks like I've got myself a family. I love you too." He was very serious saying it.

As the ladies were getting up, they moved two large tables together, to have sitting room for all present, including the children.

When the turkeys and the many foods began to crowd the table, Halge approached Andrew and asked, "Mind if we sit together? I have the feeling that perhaps we have a lot to converse about."

He smiled at her, "I was hoping the same..." He helped her to sit down and then took a seat himself. He said, "I have to apologize again, you simply seem so familiar to me, but... Well... Living on my own, the emotions get away at times."

Some time later he explained, "Having met the five ladies and getting along so beautifully with all of them means a lot to me. We simply hit it off right."

Before they all began to eat, Hety said with a grin in the direction of Andrew, "Bon appetit! I seem to remember that a certain man greeted us at one time, while we were having our lunch in the woods." They all grinned with a knowing nod.

Surprised, Halge asked, "You also speak French?"

"No," he replied with a laugh, "I just happen to know this one because you can't say it in English."

During the long eating procedure, not much was said, but Andrew noticed that Julia had an occasional long glance at him and he thought, 'From where do I remember that face?' Suddenly then, it came to him... She looked exactly like his mother!

The so very busy Hony said, "You stay right on your seats for the dessert, then you can move back into the living room. We have it all under control with the dishes. We're well organized," she grinned.

Halge asked Andrew, "You're not having any of this wonderful pie?"

Shaking his head, "No, being into nutrition for some years, I know what's good for this old body."

"Oh," she called out, "I'm into that too, but indulge here and there," she smirked at him.

"Well, my dear lady," he smirked back at her, "you're still young and beautiful and very well padded, as I see it. Your body probably likes those little indulgences and does rather well."

"Oh you," she laughed, while putting her hand on his arm, "the way you said that..."

With a rather serious voice she said some time later, "We seem to have so much in common and I would suggest to come together. But you probably heard about my husband... We love him very much, so we keep him at home, although his mind is gone..."

Later, after they had seated themselves in the living room, Halge continued to explain, "We couldn't bring it over our hearts to place him in one of those homes, so we have a nurse to look after him properly. The children miss him, and now they still can speak and put their arms around him, although he does not understand nor react." Then, "It's only good we're well off and have no financial pains, so to speak."

After some deep thought, she began to reveal her life's story: She ran away from a foster home when only thirteen in Germany. On the street and often living off people's garbage, she made it to France where she worked in the vineyards for two years in the south. Then, hearing about Canada, she smuggled herself into a container loaded with wine for the New World. Half-starved, she arrived in Montreal, but it was winter and very cold, much too cold for her flimsy dress. Asking for a job in a department store, she was discovered by Leonard, her husband.

Only seventeen years of age at the time, he took her in, so to speak. He was very kind to her and not abusive at all. They went to Toronto where he lived at the time. Now she had to learn English and he taught her about the Jewish religion, which she began to like.

After two years, he asked her to become his wife and they were very happy. His business brought them first to Vancouver and then to Vancouver Island, where she had her first child, Julia.

Her husband planned everything in their lives, even the children they wanted to have. But eventually, they lost interest in the Jewish faith. Perhaps now the time had come, to find something, some belief, the children also might be interested in. One day she spoke to Getta, her neighbor, and through her she also got to know the other ladies and what they believed in.

She finally said, "And now I meet you. Perhaps you have something of interest for me. I'm very much attracted to the love you have for each other. It really warms my heart."

Putting his hand on her arm and nodding with a smile, he said, "I just might've something of interest for you..." all the while he was nodding. "But let me tell you about my life first, which is nothing in comparison with yours." His mother was German born and his father from the today's Czech Republic. However, he hardly got to know them because they both were killed in an airplane crash when he was only five years of age. So his grandfather raised him all by himself, but very old already, he died when Andrew was just nineteen.

There was enough money for him to go to college and become an engineer. He always had a good job with the government until a few months back, when he took early retirement.

When still young, he was married, but it lasted only three years because his wife — as she explained their break-up — found a man she really loved. He finished his story with the words, "It was a blow to me, thinking that our marriage was good enough to last forever. But, as young as I was and as naïve, I connected love with good sex only."

A moment later, he added, "But since then I did a lot of growing on all levels of endeavor and discovered real love. The gift from the five ladies today was proof, we six have a love for each other I never experienced before. It is the love of soul, of course, which one cannot dress in words, but only deeds. One feels it with heart and soul and it goes both ways." He had become very serious.

Halge replied, "Perhaps I have, or should I say we — meaning my children also — have met the right people." They had a long look into each other's eyes... Was it the communication of their souls?

Then Andrew asked out of the blue, "How does reincarnation appeal to you?"

Puzzled, she replied, "I don't know a thing about it."

He patted her hand and said with his smirky grin, "On our hike tomorrow we shall introduce you ... if you want to hear."

*   *   *

Chapter 4

An Arduous Hike

On Christmas Day, Hony was calling Andrew, while he was soaking in his bathtub. He grabbed the phone and said, as if he knew who was on the line, "In this downpour we can't go…"

There was a hesitation, then Hony called out, "How did you know I was calling?"

"I didn't," he laughed, "but one of you girls must, who else would?" Then, "Hey, I need somebody to rub my back, as I'm taking a bath…"

"Be serious for a moment, Andrew, for tomorrow they also forecast rain. So, the day after Boxing Day, on Thursday, we might be able to go. Too bad, Halge's children really looked forward to it."

After a long thought, he answered, "So did I, Hony … and wished I could visit them, but… I can't do that, it wouldn't be appropriate. With this heavy rain I also have to plan for a different hike, because some of the old trails will be flooded. Will you phone the other girls and the Copperfields? Let me know on Thursday please. By then it'll probably be cleared up."

Hardly out of the tub, Hety called, "Some rain, hey...?"

He answered, "The weatherman might've us two in mind..."

"Oh, Andrew, I was thinking the same. I feel like a schoolgirl, though, sneaking up to your place... Is twelve o'clock all right?"

"I'm holding the door open, Hety."

Later, in his arms, she whispered, "I can't help it, Andrew, I don't feel right... I mean, we girls are so close and... What if one of them asks, 'Are you seeing Andrew?' What do I answer, 'No,' that would be a lie, or do I say, 'Yes, we're hiking together... In this rain...?'" Her laugh sounded artificial.

He led her into the living room, where they sat down on the sofa. "You're right, of course, but we're no saints either, Hety." Then, "In the beginning it looks all so easy, but then the conscience knocks on the door of our... of our soul, I guess. I do understand you very well. After all, how far does our responsibility go? Only to ourselves? The girls and you are such good friends and since Christmas, I feel as if I'm one of you."

A bit later, he continued in the same vein, "Love, that is true love as in our case is a beautiful thing. But ... perhaps it also gives us responsibilities. After all, we're not living together, nor are we married."

With her arms around him, she whispered and suggested, "Let's make this our last time, then we can meet the others with a clean shirt."

Later on at the house door, she said, "I'm glad we've made this decision," and she inhaled deeply.

He answered, "True love also requires discipline

55

... that is, self-discipline, and not to be selfish."

After a last strong embrace, a sure-footed Hety walked toward her vehicle, and before entering it, raised her hand with a smile. He threw her a last kiss.

Back inside the house, Andrew thought, 'That woman... She sure taught me a big lesson today. Let's face it, Andrew, old boy, you didn't feel all that comfortable either, although you really love her, but so you do the others.'

Some time later then he thought, 'I better get myself a woman I can marry. Those five sure have inflamed something in me.'

* * *

Next day, Boxing Day, Halge phoned Andrew to his surprise, and she asked, "Mind if we come for a visit? You see, the children made a Christmas present for you and want to present it personally. Something inspired them, and with this rain pouring down, they stuck their heads together early yesterday and... Well, I don't want to take the surprise away... They're standing here with me and are wondering."

First he didn't know what to say, then stuttered kind of, "But... I mean... They hardly know me..."

She replied, "You have to know us better to understand, Andrew. When things start rolling, so to speak, we begin to do something about it. And your story, the way you say things, even seeing the children as an equal, calling you by your first name, leaves an impression of a very positive nature. And here they began by making you a Christmas gift. So..."

"Please ... please, say no more, my dearest Halge," he called out excitedly, "no more explaining is necessary. You good people are down my line... First I dis-cover the five ladies and now you... Somebody behind the scenes must be at work. I'll give you my address..."

"We've got it already from Hony. Will one o'clock be OK?"

With a laugh he replied, "Yes, of course, I will be at the door." After he had hung up, he tapped with his fingers on his forehead, a habit when he was excited. Then thought, 'Mother and children will come...'

He went into the kitchen to prepare his lunch, thinking, 'This rain definitely is creating something very positive in my direction.'

*   *   *

When Andrew saw the Copperfield car turn into his driveway, he rushed out with a big umbrella and greeted them, "Welcome to my home! I should've brought two umbrellas..." But the children ran under the roof-covered porch and Halge grinned, "It's only water... Look at them. They hardly can wait to show off their creation."

With both adults under the umbrella and walking toward the house, he said, "You know this rain has started something very exciting and good, and I like it."

On the porch, Andrew said to the children, "All right, you guys, beside the entrance you noticed a rotating brush in the floor for your shoes to be cleaned. If you will push that button there on the wall, it will turn and clean shoes, meaning the shoes will stay on in the house."

Shaking her head in wonder, Halge said, "What a wonderful device... We should have one like that at our place." Then she reminded the children, "OK, children, your shoes are clean now. Mind if I get my shoes on the brush too?" Only reluctantly they backed away.

Inside the house, and with their jackets and coat off, they entered the living room. With expectation in his voice, Andrew said, "I hardly can wait... And to begin with, we hardly know each other... Well..."

"If you just sit down," Julia cut in, "then we'll explain." She continued, "When we saw the ladies and what they gave you because they loved you, we thought about it at home... We also like you a lot and Louise said that we also can make you something. So we three painted a picture," and she took a paper off a 2-1/2 x 2-foot-sized framed picture.

Lost for words, Andrew looked at it for several minutes. With blinking eyes he said then, "Obviously, Mrs. Copperfield, your children are wonderful artists... And you all painted it together?"

"I did the box camera with the string," Louise explained.

He knelt down in front of her and said, "You liked my story, hey?" She nodded. "You know what part of it was very much true? I dearly loved the girl and wished I could've had her picture."

Getting up again, Andrew laughed, "It's the story of my life. I had to wait until now to find love." Then, "Oh, I simply love that picture... The wonderful ideas you had with the flowing creek, the forest and the hills... The old house there and the camera on the ground, all beautifully put down with the brush... And doing it with watercolor, something not easy to do. You are very, very creative. And I thought I was, when I build all kinds of stuff in my workshop. But from where did you get the frame so fast?"

Floyd explained, "It was an old picture nobody liked. So Mom said to use the frame for your picture."

At a loss what to say next, Andrew asked haltingly, "I kind of wonder whether I could thank you by putting my arms around you...?"

Louise took the initiative by motioning him down and saying very quietly into his ear, "I also love you, Andrew." He gave her a big squeeze with tears in his eyes.

After he had hugged the other two also and wiping his eyes, he said to Halge, "I envy you."

Coming to life then, he said, "Hey, let's find a wall to hang it up on. As you can see, there is not much space left here in the living room. In what room, I wonder, would it be best? I mean, where can it give me the biggest inspiration? I see a lot of love in your picture..." Then, "Would it be all right to have it in my workshop? You see in there I'm more creative than anyplace else, and there is a lot of heart and soul in what I conceive and invent."

"Can we see your workshop?" Floyd asked immediately.

Getting up, he said, "OK, let's go." And they all followed him.

"Hey, you've got a scooter..." the boy called out at once, "and with big wheels, Mom."

Naturally, there was a lot to look at, and they all wondered about the large workshop with so many tools. After all the nosy questions had been answered, he said, while tipping his finger to his chin, "I think your beautiful picture will go into this room, right there above my designer table, where a lot of my creations come to bear. Your picture will be an inspiration to this knucklehead of mine," grinning, he knocked on his head. "So will somebody be so kind and get it, to be put up forthwith." While Louise held it up, he nailed it to the wall, under the happy eyes of the three youngsters, and their mother too.

Back in the living room later on, and sitting beside each other on the sofa, Halge pointed out quietly, "You're a hit with them..."

He simply answered, "I'm so grateful you came," and he patted her arm.

After the children had quieted down, getting up, Andrew walked to a large glass-covered cabinet. Turning around again, he said, "I don't know whether this is the right time to show some of my pictures... Well, here it goes. You will understand my concern." He took out two picture albums and placed them on the table. "If you all come around and see for yourself."

With them all crowded around, he began to turn the pages of the first album. Suddenly Halge called out, "That's you, Julia!"

"No," Andrew replied, "it's my mother." Turning several other pages, he said, "Look at some of those old pictures... This great aunt of mine from my mother's side, how does she look to you?"

"That's me!" Halge called out with even more excitement. "But how is that possible?"

Halge couldn't help but suggest, "Which means that we're all related, doesn't it?"

"No, my dear lady," came the sober reply, "we're not related in the physical sense, but spiritually we are."

After the albums had been closed and all were

60

back on their seats, breathing deeply, Andrew said, "What I'm going to tell you now might come as a shock, but I don't know any short cut way to explain all this. I had planned to introduce you slowly, but this rain and bringing the beautiful picture to me, kind of changed my plan. Some invisible hand, it seems, was at work, which will happen sometime. We have no control over it."

Little Louise had come to her mother to sit on her lap to be close.

"So here it goes," he began: "We all have a soul within our body. It's a god-like entity and without it we would not be alive. Soul is eternal. It never dies. How can that be, you might ask? That's where rein-carnation comes in. Soul goes from lifetime to life-time for the purpose of learning lessons. When we die, it is only the physical body, while soul lives on, until the next opportunity presents itself, to enter a new body as a baby."

After some deep thought, he continued, "From in between the physical life, many of us know each other. Why, when I saw you first, Halge, I couldn't tear myself away with my eyes ... because as soul I recognized you as an old acquaintance. Believe me, my heart was pounding. It was hard to control. We also might've been very close in a former lifetime, something we do remember as soul."

Suddenly Julia called out, "And I know you also, Andrew, because I was your mother," she began to cry, comforted by her mother, holding her close.

Getting up, Andrew said to Floyd, "Mind giving me a hand in the kitchen? I think we all would like to have some juice." Out of earshot of the others, the boy said, "Maybe we're related too, Andrew?"

"It wouldn't surprise me."

Changing the subject then, the boy asked, "I like the scooter you have with the big wheels. You think I could have one too? I mean, is it hard to make?"

Andrew put his arm around his shoulder and laughed, "You can have mine, I walk all the time now. Something similar they have today in specialty stores, so we'll get one for your little sister. But for the moment, it's between us, hey?"

Back with the glasses and a big jug of juice in the living room, Andrew suggest, "Get a book from Hony. I forgot who still has mine. In there you will find a very good understanding on how this works. I know a mother, also very new to this subject, who is reading aloud to her children out of it. As a single mother, she's telling me that they're like new with this knowledge. When the ladies and I say that we love each other, it is as souls, of course, the most noblest of all loves."

Giving the filled glasses to them all and sitting down himself, Andrew said, "Love is the most important thing in our lives. Without it we have wars and violence, which seem to be the norm today, listening to the news. However, love has also two sides to it. The love we give without expecting a return and the selfish and dominant love, like the mother who wants to keep the child to herself, although the boy or girl is already twenty years old. In a case like that, love can be very binding and it becomes negative."

After a few sips out of the glass, he continued, "Look how long it took me to find real love, and most of all, to be able to give love. My heart and soul are so jubilant, one simply feels it and is filled with it. I rest my case," he grinned.

Then Floyd whispered to his mother, and she called out, "You didn't, Andrew?"

"I hardly use the scooter anymore," he gave his smirky grin, "besides, I've something new on my mind. With the picture hanging there now, new ideas come into play, ha ha."

"Before we're getting off this reincarnation business for the time being," Andrew began once more, "I want to ask you whether you ever heard the term karma?"

Raising her shoulders, Halge said, "I heard about it, but not much more."

"Karma and the Law of Cause and Effect," he explained, "are responsible for everything in our lives. Why are we, why are the ladies and I put together again? It's not an accident! As long as there is something to be worked out between us, called karma — to give our example again — we can be very sure that we will be put together again, to work it out, the long arm of God makes sure of that. Our society nor our religions, unfortunately, do not acknowledge that. A curtain is drawn over people's minds, of course. If all past lifetimes were known already to a small child — when violent acts were committed in a former life — mental disorders would be the result for sure. In this lifetime they're father and daughter, in a past lifetime he was a buccaneer and she his slave. You see what I mean?"

A moment later he went on, "As a soul, however, even in a very small child, we're already mature and adult, through the eyes of our physical understanding. But from a soul's point of view, there're different stages of maturity, all depending on past lifetime karma. As soul we know many things, we have not the slightest concept of with our minds. You've heard about our intuition. It's soul trying to speak to us. Oh," he suddenly shook his head, "I probably have gone too fast and too far already. There's so much to tell and I don't know when to stop."

Halge stood up to look out of the window, then said, "It stopped raining. It's not too late for a little walk outside."

"Yes," he replied, "the fresh air might do us some good."

They walked around several blocks with the two small children, Louise and Floyd, way ahead with Andrew's scooter. However, Julia also wanted to ride it. Now it seemed a good implement to get the children off the perhaps painful and strange subject.

"What about my husband and me ... and all of us?" Halge suddenly asked.

Andrew wondered how far he should go with an answer, but said, "I'm almost sure that his soul is already in the other worlds, so to speak. From there he's trying to let you know that he's very much alive and OK. But how does he contact you? Often enough it's a predicament because the family members only see the body. There's one medium to communicate with the departed though, and that is through our dreams. Before you go to sleep, say out loud that you're very much aware now of the dream connection to the other worlds. Then have a dream journal on your night table to record your dreams when you have them because often enough you already have forgotten them when awake. This too is a very vast subject, not to explain 'on the run', so to speak."

Hooked into his arm, she searched out his hand and said with a smile at him, "I like you a lot, Andrew."

He didn't answer, but thought, 'There're at least 30 years between us,' and he inhaled deeply. To him it was more than just a liking for her.

Entering his home again, and the telephone rang. It was Hony, who said, "The weather is clearing up, Andrew. We can have our hike tomorrow."

"Good idea," he replied. Then said, "I forgot to whom I gave the book to, by Dr. Newton. You think Halge could borrow yours for a while? They're here right now and we did a lot of talking…"

Immediately Hony asked, "Could I bring it there right now and pick up the other books you have for me…? You know the books I mean?"

"Yes, Hony, you think the time is ripe?"

"Andrew, please…"

"OK, OK, I'll have them ready. In fact, I already have them in a box and you can keep them for good."

The children greeted her on the porch, to watch her cleaning her shoes with the rotating brush. Little Louise said, "Andrew is making us one too."

"He is, hey?" Hony called out. "Then I want one too." Inside and with her coat off, she handed the book to Halge and said laughing, "That man is keeping us all in a spell… Only a week or so ago I was very dissatisfied with my life, and he practically changed that within a day."

Andrew wanted to object by holding up his hands, but she simply said, "I don't care what you say,

Andrew, it is the truth."

That praise didn't make him feel very comfortable at all, and he thought, 'That Hony is simply talking too much.'

There was a lot of talking going on for the next half an hour, but it wasn't the man of the house who did the talking. When they finally readied themselves to go and he helped them into their coats and jackets, he couldn't help saying, "You all have been the nicest happening to me... And I will treasure that beautiful picture. It's too difficult to dress in words."

Hony gave him a squeeze and simply said, "Love..." Then she said, "Thanks for the books," and her eyes looked steadily into his.

Outside on the porch, Louise took Andrew's hand and said, "I love you too, Andrew."

So he lifted her up and kissed her on the forehead, as tears made their way down his cheeks.

There wasn't too much room for the scooter in the Copperfield car, so Hony said, "Here, put it in mine, I'll take it to your place."

Andrew waved with a happy heart, as they drove off, and he whispered, "See you tomorrow."

* * *

Two cars with ten people were driving down Thain Road first and then turned onto Kingburn. At the end they turned for a short run to the right and parked the vehicles there. Andrew explained, "This is the entrance to a new little park right down to the Koksilah River."

Then he warned the children who were running ahead, "Slow down, children, please. It's very steep at times and you might fall. Let's not begin our walk with an accident."

Talking to the ladies then, he said, "As you might've observed, they just did this trail properly last year, and even put in a few stairs for an easier descent."

Pointing down to the children, Halge said, "See those three? It's like heaven to them. We should do this more often."

Standing behind and leaning against a sturdy wooden railing, they all looked down the steep embankment into the rushing waters of the Koksilah River. "When the water is low," Andrew enlightened them, "one can walk along the water down below and even jump from rock to rock to the other side. I must've done that more than a hundred times."

"How come we never have been down here?" Hety asked.

"You have to work during the week. And ... there has to be some love for nature ... and the desire to explore," Andrew gave his smirky grin.

A bit later, he explained, "Down the river from here you get to the fish ladder, where there is a deep pool to dive into from a high rock. The water is too cold for me and I did it only once. It was great fun, however, for three boys, who were with me at the time, and I practically had to tear them away."

After they all had filled their eyes with the beautiful and wild sight, Andrew suggested, "Today we'll go up river, but have to stay on the upper trail. Will you lead the way, children?" He pointed into the direction. "But be careful, please, it's not used very often. There might be some snags and fallen trees in the way."

Always in front, Floyd asked Andrew several times, "Which way now?"

He made it a point, to let the boy decide for himself by saying, "Take a tall tree in the distance in the general direction, then meander yourself toward it, never as the crow flies. Be agile like a deer. Some day I'll show you how to use a compass, always toward a distant tree to the next, the in-betweens are never straight."

It was rather arduous walking, with a lot of fallen trees across the old trail. Obviously, nobody had done any clearing since the last storm. Everybody helped to lift little Louise over the hurdles.

Some thirty or so minutes on the way, Andrew called out suddenly, "Hey, do you see the blue ribbon way ahead on the tall bushes? I put it there three years ago." He showed his smirky grin, meaning there was something to be expected. "Let's see what you'll discover there?"

Inspired now, Louise wanted to do her own walking and climbing over trees. She insisted not being helped. Andrew couldn't help but whisper to Halge, "She's a jewel ... just look at her."

At the blue ribbon, Floyd called out, "We don't see anything here, Andrew, so what now?"

"Stay right there, young man," came the reply with a raised finger, "and wait 'til we're all there."

"Boy, this is really something," Hety voiced her delight, "I just love it."

They all agreed and then impatient Julia asked, "What now?"

With everybody present, Andrew pulled a little penlight out of his pocket and asked, "All right, all of you, what will we do with this light now? I suggest that you all have a very good look around..."

Suddenly, Angela called out with a rather puzzled question, "What's that black hole there...? Is it a cave?"

Laughing, Andrew gave her credit, "You have very good eyes, Angela. Indeed, it's a cave!"

Still laughing, he asked them, "Who is going to be first in?" Then with more laughter, "Come on, you children... If there was a bear or mountain lion in it, it already would've bolted out for sure."

With her head up, Halge took the penlight from him and moved toward the dark hole with no word, although her steps were rather hesitant. Everybody, but Andrew, was holding their breaths it seemed.

Once inside, she began to laugh, which made the children rush after their mother, and the spell of fear was broken. With them all inside, they had a good look, following the beam of the penlight, and laughed and laughed. It was only thirty-five yards into the rock, and empty, of course.

When they were all outside again, Andrew said with his old grin, "You know how often I was here? At times with snow on the ground, hoping to see the footprints of a cougar. I was hoping to see one dash out... I had my camera ready. But they never did me the favor."

Hety said laughing, "You're making this up again, Andrew."

Rather serious this time, he answered, "No, I am not, Hety." Then, "I must've been here at least twenty times, but no animal was ever in there and came out." All but the children were shaking their heads. A new Andrew stood in front of them, it seemed.

As they were on their way again, Louise turned around and said to Andrew, "Now we're all your friends, and you don't have to go here anymore alone."

He put his index finger to his lips, touched her nose with it, then answered, "Yes, my little one, you're so right. Now I have you, your brother and sister, your mother and the five ladies as real friends. It's so wonderful." Obviously, she was thinking about the danger of being alone in the forest with so many wild beasts.

There was a lot more difficult walking and climbing, at times too arduous for the little girl, and everybody helped her to get over the hurdles. One also could hear a lot of laughs, until they reached a trail which looked more like a road.

"Some thirty or so years back, I drove down here with my car," Andrew explained. "Today they have gates and dug ditches all over, to prevent cars from coming here." Pointing to a narrow trail, he said to the children ahead, "Turn right now, where it will lead us to the river below."

Seeing a red ribbon a bit later, he said, "As you can see, other people have been here too. We might as well go all the way down to the river. It's very interesting there, as you will see. But children, please, be very careful and hang onto Louise, Julia. It might be very slippery after this rain."

Andrew waited until they all were standing together on this huge rock to answer their questions. Pointing up, he explained, "That's a monastery. It can be reached by Riverside Road from Cowichan Station. I've been up there a few times for a visit. I know Brother Glen for some time and we two have hiked together. When the water is low enough one can get across by jumping from rock to rock. When they're at home, they come out and wave. They also have a dog... And there he is right now, but we can't hear him barking because of the loud rushing water below."

Then, "They're all working in Duncan now, as far as I know, probably the reason nobody is at home at the moment. Hey, let's take some pictures, but hang onto each other, please. It's very steep down into the water and very cold."

There was a lot of laughing, with Andrew trying to get into the picture himself, having only thirteen seconds with the self-timer to join them.

Before they climbed up the steep hill again, he explained, "When the water is very low, one can walk right along it on top of some rocks. There I also discovered another half water-filled cave, but it's very difficult to get at. I know at least five more caves, hacked into the rocks by miners many years ago, but they only found iron and not gold, what they were after. Those mine shafts are never very deep and actually are easy to find on the other side of the river high up the mountains."

On the road again, Halge aired her concern about Louise, and she said without her hearing it, "She's tiring..."

With a laugh, Andrew asked the little one, "Would you like to ride on my back?" She simply nodded. Then he suggested, "We can whisper something nice to each other."

Easy going now, the women began to sing. It sounded like beautiful music to the man and he expressed his pleasure by saying, "Oh you girls are warming my heart."

At the cars, everybody was glad to get off their feet again, and Andrew said, "Perhaps we overdid it, hey? I..."

Hony interrupted him with the words, "Not so. We had the most wonderful time of our lives. Maybe I should just speak for myself."

"No no, no no," Halge raised her hands, "I, that is this family agrees with you, Hony."

Then Floyd commented, "I've never seen a cave before. It was fun to me, Andrew."

With a grin, Hony called out, "Pizza time, at my place."

Pulling the cell phone out of his pocket, Andrew suggested, "You want to order it from here?" It caused a hearty laugh by all, because of his quick reaction.

Before entering her car, Halge said, "Let me con-tribute at least some, now we're eating at your place again and..."

Hety replied, "You already do, Halge, by joining us with your children. We're still in the happy Christmas spirit, so let's prolong it for a little while longer."

All agreed while Andrew was clapping his hands and said laughing, "Pizza, here we come again... May I offer you the phone once more, Hony...?"

"Gimme that thing," she pulled it out of his hand under everybody's laughter.

Riding with the Copperfields in the car this time, Andrew said, "Your offer was well meant, of course, the girls know that too. We all are rather well off and our real friendships are more treasured than anything else."

"I do understand," Halge replied.

When they were entering Mill Bay, Halge said, "I'm going for a quick look into the house, and see whether everything is OK." And she left the car.

However, it took a long time... She did not come out of the house again, so Julia said, "I'll go and see." When she appeared, her face looked almost grave and she uttered, "Our father has died, we have to stay here now."

Following the children into the house, Andrew confronted Halge, and he whispered, "What can I do to help? What about the children? I could take them, you know."

Taking one of his hands, she said, "It had to come, and now it is reality. Oh, there're so many things to be done..." Then, "I will have him cremated, before all his relatives come from Israel. They won't like it, but he is <u>my</u> husband."

Andrew said then, "I better phone the ladies. They'll pick me up. You want me to drive the car into the garage?"

"Yes, please do," was her absent-minded reply.

Before leaving the house, Andrew said to Julia, "Please tell your mother again that I will help, no matter what it is."

She seemed very level-headed and replied, "I know you will, Andrew... Floyd and Louise are with our father right now." Nodding, he took her hand and patted it, then left the house.

* * *

73

Chapter 5

Vengeance on the Innocent

After Andrew had driven the Copperfield car into the garage, he began to walk toward Hony's place, only five blocks away, so why call the ladies to pick him up. But hardly underway, he thought, 'I better inform them before they begin to worry about my whereabouts.' Pulling the cell phone out of his pocket, Hety answered, "We wondered about you guys...?"

"I'm on my way walking, because Leonard Copperfield has died in his sleep. I'll tell you when I get there in a few minutes."

However, soon Hety came zooming with her car alongside and opened the door for him to jump in. She said, "Poor kids, but it was to be expected... What can we do, Andrew?"

"Slow down, Hety, there is no rush at the moment," he said in deep thought. "Let's put our heads together and see..." he tried to calm her down.

With them all in Hony's living room, everybody seemed to have some suggestion how to be of help to the Copperfields, but Mira had the best idea, "They still have to eat. Why not bring them a pizza, which should be here any time now."

On their way to the Copperfield place, Hety and Andrew were to deliver the pizza, not that they were too easy about it... Would it be the right thing to do? After all, they probably had other things on their minds, than eating...

However, greeting them at the door, Halge said, "Oh, you beautiful people! I simply could not collect myself and prepare a meal for all of us. That you thought of us... Come on in, we'll be sitting in the kitchen, while the nurse is dressing my... the body properly. She insisted to do it on her own. The children are taking it remarkably well."

Entering the kitchen, she said to the children, "Look what they brought us..." Louise called out, "A pizza..."

Then Halge invited them, "Please, do join us. And please, don't be concerned too much. We're over the first shock now. Sit down, please."

Andrew remembered then, "The girls are kind of concerned and wondering, perhaps I should give them a ring." He walked into the hall where he picked up the phone, to give the four ladies a report on the situation.

While eating quietly, Louise informed the visitors, "Now we know for sure that our father is in heaven."

They all nodded and Andrew bent down to her and said, "Yes, indeed, and from there he will send you his love."

After the meal and in the hall again, Halge said quietly, "I'm not looking forward to this and with what I have to put up with soon, when all his relatives arrive here…" Then, "It will not be very good for the children because there are bound to be arguments. So, I'm inclined to take your offer, Andrew, at least Floyd and Louise should not be exposed to this,"

He replied, "I'm only a telephone call away, do not hesitate, please."

On their way out, Hety reminded Halge once more, "We're five very capable ladies, you know that by now. Even if it means giving you emotional and mental support. With our love we can overcome any difficulty. And, if it means physical support and backup, we'll give that too. Let next door Getta know." There was a strong embrace by the three.

* * *

Eight relatives had come from Israel to give Leonard Copperfield their last respects and farewell. However, at once they showed their displeasure, when they were facing a large picture of the deceased in his coffin and an urn with his ashes. When they showed their bitterness even toward the children, Halge phoned Andrew and said, "The climate in our house has become too sterile and there is no love, as we know it. Please, Andrew, help."

"I'll be there in a minute," he replied.

Well, it took a 'bit' more than a minute, but when he got there, Halge had a few bags and the two little ones ready, waiting outside the house. She said, "You can't imagine what's going on here and I'm so glad to have you and your love, Andrew. The five girls helped already with meals and their love, of course. Julia insists on staying with me. Floyd knows the way to school. Perhaps they can catch the bus. They both are taking it rather well, but too much is too much," she gave him a hug. "I'll let you know when it's over. Is there room for their bikes and the scooter?"

"We can leave the trunk open, no trouble at all," he replied. Then, "Think about our love," he took her hand and his eyes said the rest. With the bikes loaded, they soon were on their way.

They first dropped in at Hony's place, where Louise and Floyd ran into her arms. "We're staying with Andrew," the boy said matter-of-factly, and Louise added, "They argue all the time and now we will be with Andrew and won't listen to it anymore," she gave her big friend a big hug.

"I thought we'd drop in here first," Andrew explained, "so you guys know what the situation is. I hear you're helping already... It's a wonder that we all met the way we did. The invisible hand, it was Spirit bringing us together. How can we doubt it." Then, "What else can we do, but send our love to the Copperfield house. Halge is very strong and will survive any negativity. I admire Julia. She chose to stay with her mother."

A moment later he said, "We better get going and settle in. Only good I have a big house and plenty of beds. Now," he squeezed little Louise, "you will have to sleep in a big bed, and you too, Floyd. So, let's go. My neighbor's dog is probably waiting already. Around this time, I take her for a walk every day." Then to Hony, "Let's talk by phone whenever we feel the urge, hey? See you." The children waved while they drove off.

* * *

Going from room to room on the second floor of Andrew's house, Floyd finally said, "Can't Louise and

I sleep together in the same room? I mean, the rooms are so big, the beds are so big…"

Scratching his head and wondering how to answer this, Andrew asked, "Are you sleeping in the same room at your house?"

"No, we all have our own room, but here…"

"Look, Floyd," Andrew was searching for an answer and thought, 'I wish I had Halge here right now.' "You're old enough to know that men and women don't sleep in the same room, unless they're married, and…"

"But, we're only children… At home we often get undressed together in the bathroom…"

"But, you're not taking a bath together, or…?"

"No, we don't," said little Louise, "I don't want to be in the same bath with him."

Andrew finally had made up his mind and said, "Look, you two, I'm not your parent. I'm like a big brother to you. I know that much, although I never had my own children, boys and girls do not sleep in the same room. You see, we adults are preparing you for the time when you're also adults and this preparation starts when you're still young. It's that simple."

"It's about sex. I saw that once on TV."

Andrew answered with an inner grin, "You clear that up with your mother. I'm not qualified to give you a lecture on that, Floyd."

So the two took their room on each side of Andrew's bedroom, who suggested, "We can leave our doors open, if you should be afraid in your big room."

After they had unpacked their few belongings and placed them into the cabinets, Andrew said, "I think I can hear my doggy friend scratching at the door below. So, put your jackets on and I will introduce you to Hollywood."

As they were walking down, Floyd asked, "How do you mean, Hollywood?"

Laughing, Andrew replied, "That's the name they gave her because often enough she behaves like a movie actor... Well, you'll see."

When they opened the house door, she began to bark and then sniffed the children over. "We have to put her on a leash first," Andrew explained, "because she always goes after little dogs and bites them. As you also will discover, Hollywood is not very smart with only little intelligence... But we all love her and know how to handle her... Well, we think we do," he laughed.

On their way into the nearby wooded area, Hollywood suddenly bolted forward, and if it hadn't been for Andrew, the German Shepherd-sized dog would've dragged the children with her at the end of the leash. A cat had caught her eyes. She hated cats. Laughing, Andrew explained, "As you can see, our doggy is very strong, and she doesn't mind choking herself out of breath with the chain around her neck. Not very smart, hey?"

Released from the leash, now inside the woods, she dashed forward after a rabbit, which was much faster, of course. There always was something of interest to sniff and go after.

Andrew explained, "Often I take the neighbor's children here, and we do some exploring or even cutting new trails. It's a lot of fun. Later I shall introduce you to all the kids, boys and girls. Now, with you back in school, I don't see them too often. But one eight-year-old girl always comes to my place, even in the evenings. You'll meet Anna later on. She has no father and brings a book for me to read to her."

"Like us," Louise said at once. He just nodded, then went on, "She always looks so sad as if she is very lonely. Maybe you can help me to cheer her up and give your love to her."

With the dog delivered at its home again, Andrew suggested, "Let's go home and plan for our meals. You have to tell me what you eat and I'll tell you what I eat. Maybe I'll like your food and you'll like mine, then we'll mix them up."

While doing that, somebody knocked on the house door. It was Anna with a book. After the introduction, Floyd said at once, "Can we play outside Andrew? We can ride the bikes and the scooter..."

Anna seemed happy to have found two 'instant' friends. With their jackets on, they left the house.

When the phone rang, it was Hony and she explained, "They're going to a lawyer this afternoon with his will. Too bad we can't be present... I bet Halge will be glad when it's all over."

"Let's not lose our cool, Hony. What we all will do is give our love. Let's keep our emotions in control. After they have left again, we'll do our thing, if she needs help."

"Yes, yes, you're right, of course. I'll give you another ring." And she hung up.

Andrew was watching through the window, as other children from the neighborhood joined the three with their scooter and bicycles. However, now everybody wanted to ride the scooter with the big wheels because it was faster and better to control.

Floyd stood his ground though, after all, it was his scooter and he wanted to ride it.

Watching the children for a while, he came to the conclusion that the big-wheeled scooter probably would be the future transportation and plaything for most of the children. So he decided to get another two, for Anna and Louise the next day. It would be Monday with the children in school. They came in large cardboard boxes and had to be assembled. Maybe he could surprise them after school.

That late afternoon, Hony was on the phone again and reported very excited, "You won't believe this, Andrew. The will gives hardly anything to Halge... She talked to Getta over the fence and was almost in tears. Anyway, that bunch from Israel, his brothers, sisters and relatives, are packing up and will be gone in the morning. Can we do anything now already? Boy, I had a bad feeling about this..."

"So did I, Hony, but, please, let's keep calm. I have a good lawyer and I'll phone him as soon as we know more. In the meantime, I'll keep the children here under my protective roof. No use getting the little ones involved in this. I wonder how Julia is doing? I respect the girl, sticking it out with her mother."

After their supper at six, Louise and Floyd went outside again to play with their new friends. Suddenly Julia appeared at the door and Andrew asked surprised, "How did you get here? You look awful... What happened? Did your brother and sister see you?"

"No, I didn't know they were outside," she replied with a trembling voice.

After he had seated her in the living room, he

said, "I'm going to get you a glass of juice. It'll calm you down. Does your mother know you're here?"

She shook her head and then practically flew into Andrew's arms, and cried and cried. He patted her back and swayed her with soothing words, "It'll be all right, Julia, it'll be all right. There is a lot of love between us and it will give us strength, a lot of strength."

After he had given the glass of juice to her, he said, "I have an idea what might have happened. You don't have to tell me, it's too painful..."

"But I want to, I have to tell somebody..." she uttered.

"You've come to the right person," he encouraged her.

After she had emptied the glass, a calm seemed to come over her, as she began to explain, while holding one of Andrew's hands: "His brothers and sisters get most of it, and mother only gets one twentieth of all his belongings, about 20,000 dollars. We only get 1000 dollars a month for all of us," she burst into tears again.

Calmed down, she continued, "He was <u>our</u> father and <u>our</u> mother's husband... How can that be, Andrew? How can that be?"

Then she added, "And mother cannot get married again, or there will be no more income. How could he do that to us...? And I thought he loved us... That's no love, Andrew. It's not to me." With his arms around her, she felt very much comforted.

When they heard the two youngsters outside, he suggested. "Let's not tell them for the time being. I have a very good lawyer and he will look into the matter. Don't worry, remember, we all love you, no matter what, and will help with all we can."

When Louise and Floyd came in, they called out, "Julia, what are you doing here?"

"I just came for a visit to see whether you need anything. But you have a lot of new friends, I hear." Then, "Our visitors will be leaving tomorrow, but you might as well stay with Andrew for a few days because it'll take us a bit to straighten out and clean up again."

On her way out, Floyd said, "I bet they did a lot more arguing..." Then he waved, "See you Juli..."

And Louise called out, "We love you."

It had begun to darken and Andrew called after Julia. "Wait a minute, girl. It'll be too dark without a light on your bike. I'll call my neighbor to babysit for a few minutes and I'll drive you home."

But Anna's mother said, "You stay right here, Andrew. I'll drive her home. Anna sure likes her new friends. She was so happy coming home. I have a lady friend with me, so don't worry." With the bike loaded into her van, they drove off.

After the children had left for school, Andrew decided to stay put, in case Halge should phone. And so she did shortly after nine. She said, "I'm free again... Well, kind of. I hear Julia was there already, so you know the score... Oh, Andrew... Mind if I come over? I simply have to lean on somebody beside Julia... She just was wonderful, the way she stuck with me... See you in a few minutes."

"Leave a note for her, in case she should come home early," he suggested.

At his house door, she said, "In spite of my calmness again, your arms around me would give me more relief…" In his arms, she whispered, "It's your love, Andrew, and now I also can return it without a bit of guilt."

After they had settled down in the living room, she said with a shaking head, "And in all those years of our marriage, I truly believed that he loved us… What kind of love is that?"

A moment later, "But he rescued me from something much worse. So, what can I say. At least we have a roof over our heads and it belongs to us, although his relatives tried very hard to take it away from us." Then, "Oh, Andrew, those people are evil, even letting it out on the children. And now comes the hardest part. How do I tell them what their father did to us? That his love was not even skin-deep. They won't understand it."

"Perhaps I can help in that regard," Andrew suggested. "Leave them with me for the rest of the week and by using stories, I might be able to tell them slowly. Good thing they trust me. Tomorrow early I will go to Victoria and buy Louise a scooter too. It might then ease her pain somewhat. My experience with children is so limited."

Then, after some thought, "I'm going to phone my lawyer and let him talk with the lawyer who handled the will. We'll make sure that everything is within the law and done properly."

On her way out, she said, "That it had to end like this."

"My dearest Halge," he took her hand, "it never will be the end! You have three beautiful children and are still young. I've introduced you to a new spiritual concept of life, perhaps we can expand on that in the near future. I read once that our physical life is only a fraction of the whole being. That thought might give you... give us all comfort. Perhaps we can explore that together."

She just nodded and walked toward her car. But suddenly she turned around again and said, "I want to see the children in their sleep."

Inside, Andrew led her upstairs where she walked into the open doors, "The rooms are so large ..." With tears in her eyes she kissed Floyd on the forehead. A moment later in the other bedroom, she covered her daughter with the blanket again and whispered, "In her sleep she wants to be free, even from blankets. No matter how often I cover, it'll come off again." And she kissed her on the cheek.

Walking down the stairs, he couldn't help saying, "I'm so grateful you let them stay with me."

She wanted to answer, but just squeezed his arm and walked toward the house door. At the car he said, "You know where I live ... Don't hesitate."

She drove off with blinking eyes.

*　*　*

With the children at school, Andrew had driven to Victoria to buy two scooters for Louise and Anna, the neighbor girl. When the two youngsters had come home, one was almost assembled. Joining him in the workshop, Louise asked with a halting voice, "Who is that for?"

"Well," he put a hand on his chin, "I know of a little girl who simply would love to have one of her own..."

"Oh, Andrew, for me?" she called out and put her

85

arms around his neck and gave him a kiss.

Her eyes simply couldn't get enough, particularly not of the white tires. "Now I have one too, Floyd. I'll let Anna ride it also. I bet she'll like that."

Grinning about her happiness, his love burst forth and he thought, 'I missed out on that... Oh, to have children to love... But I can love her ... a lot.'

Then Floyd asked, "What's in this box, Andrew?"

"I almost forgot to tell you. That's a scooter for Anna. Then you all can ride together."

"Boy, wait until she comes over..."

After some thought, Andrew suggested, "Let's surprise her, after I've got it together, OK? Then she can ride it right away with you."

That evening, Andrew phoned Anna's mother to tell her about the scooter, and said, "Please, Joanne, let me finish what I wanted to say. Anna loves her new friends and she is so happy now. I hate to see a bleeding heart. Perhaps I can meet you outside for a moment. You see, there's something else I want to tell you."

So he passed on to his neighbor the plight the Copperfield children would have to endure. He said, "Hearing this, it should make it easier to accept my little gift for Anna. You know the very first thing Louise said was to let Anna ride hers also. And you should've seen her face of joy for her friend when I told her that Anna also would get one. Let's not judge with our adult intellect. Our children are so much more important!"

Before she turned to go back, she said, "And you had to be three times my age."

"No, Joanne," he laughed, "you had to be three

times younger."

"Oh you..." she left him laughing and with much happiness.

Fortunately, the school bus stop was only a block away. Because of the heavy rain, Andrew had brought the children there with a large umbrella. And it still was pouring after the youngsters had come home. So Andrew informed them, "Today will be story time. I still have Anna's book here and maybe you should get her. I'll bet she would like to listen also."

At that moment, she knocked on the door, and, naturally, the new scooter for their friend had to have the priority. They rushed into the workshop to have a first-hand look. Louise said with great happiness, "That is yours and this is mine."

"That is for me?" she called out, "but it's not even my birthday and Christmas is over..." It obviously was beyond her understanding.

Andrew, who had joined them, had to do some hard thinking how he could explain to a girl, whose mother was not endowed with any kind of wealth, to buy her daughter a new scooter. He began, "As you know already, Floyd's and Louise's father died a few days ago and the mother didn't want the children to be there with all the relatives arguing how to bury the body. So she sent them to me because we're good friends. Now I decided that perhaps we could have another Christmas kind of and buy Louise a new scooter, since I had given Floyd mine already. I spoke with your mother, since you're now such good friends, whether I could give you one too. Naturally, your mother liked the idea very much. Now you three have one, and they all have big wheels."

Anna simply had to try her scooter by standing on it, pulling the hand brakes and smiling. It was THE gift for her. Then she said, "Thank you, Andrew." After he had bent down, she put her arms around him, if reluctant at first. But when the other two also wanted to give him a squeeze, the ice was broken and Louise found the right words, "We love you, Andrew, you're like our father."

Walking back into the living room, Anna said timidly, "I don't have a father anymore either..."

"You also can have Andrew, can't she?" Louise said at once in her innocence.

He just gave a big nod. Nobody disputed that, and the man of the house kept quiet with an inner grin. He liked his new position rather.

Later that evening, Halge phoned Andrew, "I guess they're in bed by now."

"Of course, 'mother'," he was kidding her.

"I did a lot of thinking, Andrew, why my husband did what he did. It takes a while to explain, so you might as well sit down."

"I'm sitting," he replied.

After a long pause, she began, "He wanted to convert me to his Jewish religion, and when I still was young, I didn't object at all, after all, what did I know about any religion. So far so good. However, after Julia was born and became older, his faith did not sit well anymore with me. I didn't revolt or anything of that nature, but somehow he felt my indifference. And then the two little ones later, they picked up from Julia who told him once that she wasn't all that much interested. So, during the years before he became senile, meaning that his mind didn't operate anymore, he must've decided to simply get even with us by leaving us with hardly more than a drop in a bucket. And then he had the nerve to add that clause about me... If I should dare to get married again, even the little one thousand dollars would be cut off. That is outright evil, Andrew. It has upset Julia more than it does me. Whatever she had for her father is wiped out for good."

A few moments later, she went on, "I sure like your lawyer, the way he went to work, digging into the whole matter... But nothing can be done, it's all legal, unless I want to sue his relatives by declaring the will unsound and invalid. Julia wants me to do it, but she hasn't got a clue what a venture like that will cost. No, even if I had the money... He wanted to get even — what else could've been his motive? But I won't honk into the same horn, if I may call it that. My new life begins now without hanging onto any kind of negativity. It's simply not in my nature."

Then she became more alive by saying, "Now my children are more important and I will build on that. How are they doing? Did you say something already about their father? Perhaps you should leave that to me..."

"You might be right, Halge... After all, what will I say? I'm lost with that. I'm sure you'll come up with the right idea."

Not hearing anything, he complimented her by saying, "I think you're very wise not to react on his vengeance, it never pays. Now you're ahead of the game."

"Your words are so comforting, Andrew," and she

whispered almost inaudibly, "I love you."

After a while, Andrew said, "By the way, I have become a father figure to Louise already, and she suggested the same to her playmate Anna, who too is without a father. So, here I am, a father to three children. Floyd always agrees with his little sister." Then, "If you want to leave them for another week, it's all right with me."

Thinking for a moment, she said, "I'm settled now, so on Sunday I'll have them back. I want to get on with my life, if that is possible. Your lawyer also gave me good advice with the money. I will have to stretch it, but I'm not worried." Then, "I shall let you go now, Andrew. Having you and the ladies as real friends is more comfort to me than anything else. Take care."

* * *

Chapter 6

Divine Intervention and Love

Three more weeks had gone by in the new year of 2002, and the Copperfields had settled into a new life. Halge was thinking of finding a job to supplement her meagre monthly income. She spoke to Andrew about it, who suggested, "I could look after the children while you go to Malaspina College in Duncan and take a course in something... Perhaps a job you could do at home."

With a shaking head, she said, "What would I be able to do at home? And going to school... I haven't even a high school diploma. The only thing I'm reasonably good at is being a house mother. With these uncertain times right now, the twenty thousand dollars invested doesn't give me much extra either."

"Well," Andrew replied, "how about having a 'brain storm' with the five ladies this coming weekend? We wanted to go for another hike anyway, if the good weather holds. They all do well and might come up with a suggestion. Hony told me once that she is financially very well off and never has to work for another day. Her husband left her with enough." Then, "We'll find something for you and the children."

Andrew had been at Halge's place to repair her kitchen sink plumbing and on his way out, he said, "I can repair anything, so don't you dare call a plumber or electrician. It's a cinch for me to do it all."

While driving off, he thought, 'If I was forty, I would propose to her, but with nearly thirty years between us... No, she would say something if there was more in my direction... No, Hety and I are closer in years, although I wouldn't want to marry her. But would I marry Halge? I feel so close to her. We must've been in love ... in deep love during a past life. Perhaps Spirit will show me in a dream.'

* * *

Late that very same evening Andrew had a revealing dream shortly after he had gone to bed with a thought about Halge.

It must've been in India, going by the clothing the people were wearing. Andrew found himself to be in a harem as a woman, and there were about twenty of them. At the moment most of them were bathing, chatting and laughing. It seemed a very happy life.

The next picture showed the master of this vast establishment, a very corpulent and friendly prince, who did not misuse his subjects and made sure that nobody else did.

The next picture showed the overseer of the harem, a very good-looking man — the Halge of today — and his favorite woman was no other than Andrew — then one of the harem girls. Everybody knew about their affair, and the master of the house tolerated it. Their love for each other was true and deep. End of dream.

*   *   *

Andrew changed from the dream into the waking state. In fact, he was wide awake now. While putting his hands behind his head, he was thinking, 'I was a woman then... What year could it have been I wonder? They still seem to wear the same garments today, but India has no harems anymore. It could've been under the English rule during the eighteenth or seventeenth century.'

Smiling to himself, he fell asleep again. Waking up early at four thirty, his thoughts centered on the dream once more. While preparing breakfast, he said out loud, "So I was a woman then, but today I don't feel like a woman at all. On the contrary..."

A bit later and looking into the mirror, he said out loud again, "There's no trace of a woman in this guy's face at all." Then he continued with his thoughts, 'Of course, that could've been several lifetimes ago. When you're born a boy, you look like a man later on. When you're born a girl, you look like a woman later on. But what about Hony? What are Spirit's planes as a bisexual?'

*   *   *

There was a letter in the mail from the Czech consulate in Vancouver. A relative of Andrew's father was wondering whether a descendant of a Herding — changed into Herden — was still alive. On the phone Andrew explained that he knew so little about his father, since he was only five when his dad lost his life. He didn't even have a single picture of him. So he was given an address, if he wanted to contact this rather elderly gentleman for more information.

Although he never wrote or phoned anybody, to his surprise a man came to his door a few days later and introduced himself as Rudolph Hoppe, a lawyer from the Czech Republic, representing Mr. William Herding. His English was reasonably good and it came to bear that Mr. Herding was trying to find relatives of his youngest brother, Alfred. Alfred had left his home country because of a disagreement with his parents.

After Andrew had taken some old papers out of a dusty box and put them on the table for the visitor to review, it became almost certain that his father had been the youngest brother of William Herding. There was no doubt about it.

"Well," Andrew began, "it's probably very important to Mr. Herding to have discovered his brother's son here in Canada. In the Old Country this kind of relationship is more looked upon as old family ties. So, what are we going to do with it? He's welcome, of course, if he wants to come for a visit."

The lawyer asked, "You wouldn't consider visiting Mr. Herding? He's rather advanced in years and not in the best of health anymore."

"Last year I was in Germany, from where my mother came as a small child, but my experience from there was not very favorable. Here we smile at each other and are happy most of the time. I was glad to be home again. It might not be the same in the Czech Republic and I shouldn't judge by my German experience. Why is it so important to see a long-forgotten relative again? We can correspond or speak over the phone, but in what language will we do it?"

With a light grin, Mr. Hoppe replied, "For many

years Mr. Herding belonged to the diplomatic corps and his English is as good as yours, Mr. Herden." He had said that with some pride. "The flight is paid for, of course, unless you should decide you wanted to go by the sea."

"It's not that," was Andrew's reply, "but there must be more incentive to visit an old relative I've never seen nor heard of than just seeing each other."

"He'll make it worth your while," was the reply. "I'm not at liberty to say more."

"Let me think about it for a day," Andrew stalled. "A man around my age, well set and well off, likes to think about this kind of a venture. All my friends here are like my close relatives to me, with a lot of love going both ways. To be taken away from them, even for a week... It involves heart and soul, and it requires at least an overnight thought."

Getting up, the lawyer suggested, "Will two o'clock in the afternoon be all right?"

"That should give me plenty of time," was the answer, "I will know by then." And he led the visitor to the house door.

* * *

Swinging out of bed early in the morning, Andrew knew that he would go and visit an old relative in the Czech Republic. The message from Spirit had been very clear. Not that anybody had spoken to him during his sleep, but he knew a positive feeling about a venture when there was one.

He phoned the ladies and Halge and told them that something unexpected had come up. He would fly to the Czech Republic, the birth country of his father, where a still living uncle wanted to see him.

Unfortunately, it also meant that they had to hike without him and he apologized. He suggested to them what forest trail would be easiest to use, considering the rain of the last days.

*   *   *

Friday evening, Andrew and the lawyer, Rudolph Hoppe, entered an airplane in Vancouver, to fly to Frankfurt, Germany first, and from there to the city of Prague, the capital of the Czech Republic.

What did the two men talk about during the long flight? When Andrew mentioned that he was inspired by Spirit to accept the invitation of Mr. Herding, invariably the conversation began to center around the subject of Karma, the Law of Cause and Effect or the Law of Retribution and not to forget about reincarnation and dreams.

"It took me over fifty years to discover love," Andrew was telling the listener, "and it's not the love usually known to mankind, but in this love soul is the main participant, and it is given without expecting a return. So you see, the beautiful relationship I have with all my friends. The children particularly, not too much effected by the intellect, do feel it and return it whole-heartedly. One not only feels it, but sees it in their smiles. We know when we come into each other's orbit, because heart and soul feel it."

"You said that Spirit is responsible for everything," Rudolph Hoppe said. "Is it also responsible for my coming to you in Canada? And..."

"Of course," Andrew interrupted him. "If you believe in God, that he knows everything about us from the past, present and future, then you will also believe that God is using his agent or channel, Spirit, to go to work, what's in the best interest of all involved. It's that simple."

Andrew began to wonder how it was possible that this man beside him wanted to know all those spiritual 'things', as if he had been waiting to meet him. What about William Herding? Had Spirit also made that connection?

What Andrew didn't know was that all their conversations were recorded because the lawyer had a hidden tape-recorder on him.

* * *

In Prague Andrew was put up in a lavish hotel room and the lawyer left him with the words, "If you would like to see the sights of the city first, a taxi is waiting for you at the desk. I think Mr. Herding will be ready to receive you in two days. I will phone you first."

Andrew was on the verge of asking, "But why not today?" but an inner nudge kept him quiet. Perhaps some mystery was revealed to him, he laughed to himself.

A very friendly taxi driver was showing him all the important sights of the big city and the visitor savored the beautiful old buildings. He also visited a couple of museums. At one point he asked the driver, "You happen to know a Mr. William Herding?"

"You mean the industrialist." Which was a big surprise to the questioner. "He's a wonderful man, the way he survived the Russians by tricking them... Everybody speaks highly of him. Why, you have some business with him?"

"I've an appointment with him in a day or two."

"He also does business in the USA and Canada. I

just was wondering." Obviously, good ethics prevented him from pursuing it. And now Andrew had an idea what he was heading for.

Inside the hotel again, the visitor wished he was home because of the very cold winter with a foot of snow on the ground. He never had brought any kind of clothing for that kind of a situation. How could he ever be able to walk outside and get his workout?

The next day, Andrew was picked up by a chauffeured car at ten in the morning and driven to a huge mansion surrounded by a moat filled with water, and it still had the old drawbridge across it. The lawyer, Mr. Hoppe, was greeting him at the bottom of the wide half-round flight of stairs. He said, "Mr. Herding is anxious to meet you, Mr. Herden. Please, do follow me and come on in."

Inside a girl took his jacket and gloves, executed with a curtsy, to the visitor's inner grin.

They entered a very large room, more looking like a hall, where Andrew detected a man in a wheelchair. The two men were introduced by the lawyer and Mr. Herding said with a strong voice, "I'm glad you could make it, or should I have said, I'm glad you decided to come?" He stretched out his hand for a solid handshake. Then he motioned to a chair for the visitor to take a seat.

"How was the long flight?" he began the conversation. "Did you enjoy it?" He went on, "I never enjoyed long flights, and if it wouldn't have been for the time factor often, I would've preferred an ocean cruise."

"Well," Andrew replied, "Mr. Hoppe and I had a very interesting conversation. Unfortunately, one never finds the right vegetarian fare on any of those flights."

"We can't have that here," Mr. Herding said at once, "You must tell my cook about your food."

After the lawyer had left, Mr. Herding waved the visitor to follow him around the large room, where he pointed out pictures on the walls and at the same time explained the different relatives from the past, going back several hundred years. "Unfortunately, I don't have your father's picture and was hoping that you might be able to supply me with one."

Shaking his head, Andrew replied, "I hardly knew my parents and only have pictures of my mother and grandfather, who raised me after the early death of my parents. In any case, my ancestors don't play an important role in my life. I've learned to live in the now."

The man of the house raised his shoulders, "Obviously, our interests in that direction are very different."

After he had rolled his chair back to the former place near a large window, he said, "Mr. Hoppe is telling me that your interests are in the spiritual worlds and everything related to it. I'm a Lutheran... Do you think that some of your knowledge is compatible with my belief?"

With a grin, Andrew replied, "All religions should be compatible with each other. God has made a religion for every individual being or group of beings, only fanatics disagree with that. Since the New York terrorist attack, many people have begun to have a hard look at their own belief and religion and ask themselves, 'Where do I stand in relation go God?' To me the eleventh of September incident only has strengthened my own belief, of which I gave Mr. Hoppe a look through an outside window, so to speak."

Mr. Herding was struggling with what Andrew just had said and finally replied, "At my age you're set in your religion, if it is comforting to you. My God has helped me perhaps a thousand times because I believe in him. However, as you approach the end of your life, one begins to wonder, is it all one could've done to be established in heaven after death? There's a certain amount of fear, I don't mind to admit, whether I did everything right. The billions I've accumulated lose their value. What do I do with it after I've left this earth?"

After a few minutes of quietness, he went on, "I have to admit that we were spying on you, because everything you spoke of to Mr. Hoppe was recorded. It was not the best of ethics, I know, but I wanted to know what you thought of me. Instead you lectured my lawyer on something spiritual I never heard of. Mr. Hoppe is much more excited about it than I am. But ignorance was never part of my life. Perhaps you have some advice for this old man?"

With a grin, Andrew couldn't help saying, "It's the old story. The closer we come to death, the more fear we have about the after-life. I wish there was an easy way to give you more comfort. If you just could center your belief on the fact that the soul is eternal, it never dies. But it also has to learn many, many lessons, and the only way to do that is if soul goes through numerous lifetimes. This one lifetime theory — that's all it is to this man — doesn't make sense. Look at the early Christians. They believed in reincarnation, but the Pope disallowed it because it is something away from the physical one can see. Study the old Greek philosophers, like Plato and Pythagoras... 'Know thyself', Plato said, which means soul, of course. Soul is a Godly entity, made of the very same fibre or material, and with it it also inherits God potential, but it has to be brought out. To do that in one lifetime would not only be insufficient, but impossible. The experiences of many lifetimes are necessary to bring us to the stage of God Awareness. The Holy Spirit is God's voice, and it will guide soul in this endeavor. Perhaps I've talked too much already."

The old man was shaking his head, "No, please, I'm not closed to that concept." Then, "Will you stay for a while? My reasons to get you here were of a different nature, I must admit, but what you explain is so much more important now. What will I do with all my wealth? It will not solve anything spiritual... You also spoke of Karma and the Law of Cause and Effect. All that needs explaining."

Looking at his watch, he said, "It's already past lunch, as you call it, so let's eat first. And you must tell my cook what your fare is. I cannot have you complain about the food in my house."

Andrew thought, 'Some house, ha ha, it's like a palace.'

For lunch Andrew simply asked for a glass of water and a couple of bananas, since it almost would be impossible to ask for soya milk and kamut or spelt bread, often his fare at home. He intended to stay away from any kind of food causing his allergies to act up. It had the cook almost up in arms, and her face showed it, when she placed the glass of water and the bananas before him. What kind of visitor was this? Andrew couldn't help but laugh to himself.

Halfway through the afternoon, with a lot of explaining by the visitor, he reminded his host, "There's something like spiritual gluttony, when one wants to cram his mind with the new won knowledge. So it is best to give this subject a rest for a while. Suddenly, soul wants to know it all, which is impossible, of course."

He asked, "You mean it's soul in me to do that questioning...?"

"Of course, remember, you're soul first, the body is adopted for this lifetime. The questions you ask don't seem to come from the intellect..."

"Yes, yes, you have a way of explaining it," was the reply, "it makes so much more sense."

Then Andrew said, "I wouldn't mind to look around a bit. It's all so beautiful here. Besides, I miss my exercises. At home I walk and swim almost every day. But the clothing I brought is not for the cold winter here."

"Oh, you poor man, and I keep you in here all that time. I shall tell the ladies to get you the proper clothing, and do all the walking you want. I'm so selfish..."

* * *

After two more days, and the recommended book by Dr. Newton at hand already — it had been brought by plane from New York within a day — Andrew said goodbye to his new won relative and uncle, William Herding. What a surprise it had been, the way the Holy Spirit had gone to work on all levels of endeavor, who could doubt that. A new old man was facing the visitor now, where the word old was

102

out of place.

While ordering the flight ticket, Andrew said very determined, "I'm not going with that German airline. On my last flight from Frankfurt to Vancouver, they had no heat at all, pointing to the blankets to keep warm. No, I'm flying first to England and catch a plane from there."

"With your experience you know what's best," were Mr. Herding's words, "and, please, do remember that everything goes on my account. Just mention my name."

The goodbye was much more than cordial. It seemed a new friendship had begun, but it did not include the cook...

*   *   *

After Andrew had entered the airplane and was seated already, for the first flight to London via Leipsig in Germany, he had a suspicious look at a man. He just had entered and passed by him to one of the seats in the back.

Much aroused, he stood up again, to have another look at the man, because his intuition was gnawing on his consciousness. So, when the flight attendant walked by, he asked, "Is everybody checked out on this plane? I have this funny feeling about that man there in the back with the red cap..."

She seemed annoyed and whispered back, "Sir, all the passengers are checked out. Don't cause any commotion, please." It did not sit well with Andrew at all, but he settled down, thinking, 'Maybe I'm wrong.'

Not flying too high because of the short distance to Leipsig, the plane hardly had reached the Erzgebirge summit, when an explosion rocked the back! Suddenly everything was in a turmoil. The back of the airplane was exposed to the outside and it appeared the pilot had no control anymore when the plane dived down into the deep snow of the mountain. It all happened so fast … accompanied by screams…

The impact was hard, very hard, but it appeared that many of the passengers had survived because of the low flight and the deep snow. For a moment, everybody was stunned, then the screaming and wailing began once more.

Making his way to the front — the back was utterly in shambles — Andrew thought to speak with the flight crew, but the impact had left them all dead. The cockpit was gone. Then he noticed the flight attendant. She tried to comfort a mother with a little child.

'What now?' Andrew asked himself. Suddenly he remembered the cell phone he had in his carry-on baggage, which would come to good use in this situation.

In the meantime it had become very cold and most survivors were not dressed for this low temperature. There were plenty of blankets, and they were all in use by now.

'I will get my other jacket and a second pair of pants out of my baggage,' Andrew thought, 'and pull them over the ones I have on already. It should help to keep me warmer.'

Moments later and with the cell phone in hand, he wondered who to call? Holding it up, the flight attendant had seen it, and she worked herself from the front of the plane into his direction. A difficult task now because people were sitting all over the floor, huddling together to keep warm.

Half out of breath, she said, "Give me that phone, please, I know who to call." She was able to reach Czech authorities forthwith, to explain their terrible situation. They wanted to send a helicopter at once.

It had become so cold that everybody began to shiver, including Andrew. He was thinking about the badly hurt people. It was impossible to see any of them in this madness... Only their cries and the moaning could be heard, particularly coming from the back. Andrew thought, 'I better keep my attention on Spirit. I want to survive this ordeal, if just for Halge and the kids. Oh, I love them so much.'

Suddenly his sharp ears began to listen... They all heard a faint motor noise and soon a large helicopter came into sight to hover overhead. They had detected the damaged plane below. It had come from Germany and was in the air when their pilots heard about the tragic happening on the radio. Not knowing the location, they skimmed low over the mountain range and in only a short time had found the place of tragedy.

Trained in rescue, the copter crew went to work immediately after they had sat down. To get the badly hurt passengers aboard was a difficult task indeed, working themselves through the deep snow. When filled to capacity, they took off again, but not before they had promised to be back soon.

A minute or two later, two small helicopters from the Czech Republic landed near the plane wreck, and they took the last of the hurt people and women and children.

Hardly in the air, and another large German helicopter sat down to take the last of the passengers aboard, including Andrew. They landed at the military airport in Zwickau, Germany.

The very first thing everybody was longing for was a hot bath or shower, but the military men were waiting for them and did a wonderful job to please. They were overheaped with all the comfort in the world.

After a few hours and feeling normal again, Andrew met the flight attendant and said, "Mind giving the cell phone back to me?"

"Oh, it's you!" she exclaimed, "this phone saved many lives."

A moment later, she remembered, "Weren't you the one who warned me about the man with the red cap? How in the world did you know that he might be a terrorist?"

"My intuition told me," was his plain reply.

It seemed a puzzle to her, and she did not follow it up with more questions.

It was discovered that there had not been a single American on this flight. In the press the question was raised whether everybody was on the list of these fanatics now who did not have their religious belief? But Andrew thought that they might have been after him as a Canadian. He dropped that thought again though, not wanting to go overboard with something he did not know.

It was surprising how friendly these military men were... The cook went out of his way to get good vegetarian food for Andrew. He thought, 'Perhaps I should revise my opinion about the German people.' Many spoke English, which made it rather easy to get around. They even loaned him a flightsuit when they heard that he was missing his walks outside because of the cold. And, of course, one could see him in the pool often twice a day for a workout.

All of Europe was experiencing one of the worst winters with a lot of snow. The other side of the coin was perhaps that the deep snow on top of the Erzgebirge might've saved the survivors from certain death.

When the newspapers with the fat headlines appeared — unfortunately all in German — Andrew thought he'd better call William Herding and tell him of his survival. He explained, "From the sixty passengers, thirty-eight survived, as you might've read. It was a miracle..." Then he added, "It was Spirit, no doubt." And he told him the rest of the story.

Toward the end of the telephone conversation, Mr. Herding said, "I know you won't like this, but I'm doing it anyway because you gave me so much hope about the spiritual endeavors you revealed to me. And the book by Dr. Newton cleared up so many things... I'm a new man physically also. So here it is. I've opened a bank account for you in Canada, and please, don't refuse it. With these uncertain times we have today, it might be of help to you in the future."

Andrew was overwhelmed, but how could he refuse a gift of thanks and love. He replied, "I'm glad I could be of help to a <u>real</u> relative. Let's talk more often on the phone."

To his surprise he heard then, "You must call me William from now on, and I shall call you Andrew. Agreed?" Of course he did. It must've meant a lot to the elderly gentleman to offer his first name.

Then Andrew called Hony at home and got her out of bed. He had forgotten the ten hours of time difference. After he had explained, she called out, "Oh, Andrew, you were on that plane? How terrible... how terrible... And you are not hurt at all... It was God and Spirit, of course. The papers are full of this happening. Does it ever end? When will you be home again? We all love you..."

She would've gone on and on if he hadn't interrupted her, "Hony, your love also helped to save me and the others, the power of love. And now you must go back to sleep. I'll be back in four or five days."

"How can I sleep with that... Oh, Andrew, you survived... It was divine intervention."

One the fourth day of their stay at the military air base, a flight officer was asking Andrew, "Would you like to go to Leipzig? We can bring you there with some of the other passengers. From there it might be easier to catch a flight to London, your original goal to fly home again. After it's all over here with the press and radio, we could go tomorrow, early at seven."

"That sounds mighty good to me. I'm fed up with the news media anyway. They're dragging it out as usual."

The officer laughed, "They're not your friends?"

"No," was his stern reply.

Next day in Leipzig, the original airline had reserved a seat for him, and already at two in the afternoon, he arrived in London, to book his flight to Canada at once.

Five hours later at seven, his plane lifted into the air. Although the service onboard was excellent, the so very long flight was boring to Andrew and he was very glad when they finally landed in Vancouver.

Very tired, he phoned Hony, "I'm home again … and will find myself a bed first. I'll take a later morning flight and be in Victoria at ten thirty. Will somebody pick me up, please?"

"Yes, yes, yes, I'll be there. Sleep well and have some dreams."

"I'll contemplate the whole venture," he laughed.

"Some venture, hey?" she finished the conversation.

Next day, however, instead of Hony, Halge greeted him at the airport gate, and almost in tears, she took him into her arms and said very assuredly, "Oh, Andrew, I love you! That you made it through that terrible plane crash…"

As they were leaving the terminal, Halge, still in tears, looked at him and at the car burst out, "I don't care about our age difference…" And her arms flew around him again.

After they had parted, he grinned, "So often I thought, what do I only do with my love for that woman?" Instead of an answer, she simply kissed him.

On their drive home, she said with joy in her voice, "Wait 'til I tell the children. You don't know how much they want a dad again, and often enough they're speaking of you. I finally found a way to explain it to the little ones, what their father was all about in our last years of relationship. You know what Louise said at once? 'And now we have Andrew.' They don't know anything about age difference, but they do know about love, Andrew, and they feel it when it comes across from you."

After they had turned on the highway up island, Halge said, "By the way, I had a letter from Israel, a lawyer was writing that he had some inheritance waiting for me. It could be a trick by his brothers and sisters. I don't trust this at all. And flying there...? And the next thing I know, the airplane is blown up. No, I think I'll stay put. What do you say, Andrew?"

"One thing I've learned in my fifty-nine years, is to never rush into anything," he replied. "If there is no deadline, let's contemplate on the matter for a few days or a week. Spirit will give you an answer, if you listen and keep your mind open. Another thing I've learned in my life, never to generalize... Not every plane we fly will be blown up from now on. And his brothers and sisters wouldn't use a lawyer to get to you. Go to their consulate and find out about his validity, whether he is known to them. Not all Israelis are bad, Halge. You just met the bottom of the barrel, as the saying goes."

After a moment, she took a hand off the steering wheel and searched out one of his, "Your wise words are very comforting. I think this family will do very well with you."

Much later and arriving at Andrew's home, she held onto him and said, very assured, "I don't have to contemplate on this nor do I generalize, Andrew... I want you to make love to me."

"You mean now?" he looked surprised... Was she serious?

"Yes, Andrew," she said with a pounding heart. "I never had a say in this and always was told... There was no love."

Holding both of his hands, she whispered, "With

you now I feel free to say what I crave from the bottom of my heart and soul ... your love ... your physical love, Andrew."

With arms around each other, he looked deeply into her eyes and couldn't help saying, "I see soul in you... We remember and want to make love."

After they had left the car and stepped onto the porch, he had a long look into her eyes again and said, "By God, we will make love with love."

Inside the house, she said with a free heart, "And I want to scream..." A slap on her bottom was his reaction. It made them both laugh with joy.

*   *   *

Chapter 7

A New Husband and Dad

After they had parked the car in front of Halge's house, Hony came out and aired her surprise, "What took you so long?"

But looking at their happy faces for a moment, she had second thoughts and followed it with the words, "Don't tell me. I can see. Oh, I'm so happy for you two."

Her next reaction was toward Andrew. She simply had to put her arms around him and said under tears, "Oh, Andrew, to have you back... We all love you..." He was just swaying her and gave his love.

After they had parted and she had dried her tears with his hanky, she took Halge's hand into hers and said, "You're so fortunate... I got the kids into bed. It had become too late to stay up for your arrival. They wondered that it took you so long, and when Julia suggested that you two probably went to Andrew's place first, it satisfied them and I could tuck them in."

Inside the house, Hony said with a quiet voice, "You know how much I envy you two? But where the real love falls, it falls…" Then, "Well, I don't really envy you, but I do love you both with all my heart and soul."

Andrew said, "Halge and I talked it over, whether we should live together or not. Perhaps we should let the children have a word in the matter. Often they know this kind of thing better, still closer to soul. At times our intellect is in the way," he grinned.

"And now, Hony, will you be so kind and drive me home. We came here first to let you know, as we don't intend to make a secret out of our love and what we intend to do."

Before they left, Hony put her arms around Halge and said with blinking eyes, "I don't have to tell you what you'll get with this man… He might be old in years, but is very wise and full of love." With that she took her coat and said, "I'll pick up my other stuff tomorrow. Let's go, Andrew." On their way out, she threw a kiss to Halge.

Arriving at Hony's house, she asked, "I couldn't ask you to come in for a few minutes at this late hour?"

"I'm wide awake, Hony, and wouldn't mind a late chat and a tea."

Sitting in the kitchen, with her preparing the brew, she said, "I don't want to comment on you two, but to say that little Louise sees you as her father already."

"Yes, I know," he replied. "When they stayed with me, she already had tagged me that way."

Then Hony said, "Since I've met you and certainly since I've read the books on sex you gave me, I come more and more to the realization that I most likely will have to do without a mate for the rest of my life. Is that the lot of a bisexual, I ask you?"

As he was sipping the hot tea slowly, his mind generated a deep feeling for her and it effected his heart also, as he asked himself, 'What has Spirit got in mind, to let this woman be born as a bisexual?' Out loud he said, "To answer that, Hony, I would have to dig into your past lifetimes, which I can't. We're so limited in this respect... With all the things we know so far and believe in, we're way ahead of our fellow men, so, what do we do with what we know?"

After he had emptied his cup, he continued, "Even if we knew from a past life why you have to put up with this condition in this body, would it help us in any way? Except perhaps to satisfy our curiosity. You could play with your imagination and think of all the reasons, something you probably have done already a hundred times over with heart and soul."

A bit later, and after she had waved him into the living room, he said, "In a way this old guy you're with right now had to put up with something similar, when I think about your plight. For many years I only associated love with sex. When I finally came to the wake-up realization — that's what it was in my case — that real love is of heart and soul, I was old, Hony. There were not many women around my age who wanted out of marriage what I envisioned. You don't know what it did to me when you said you didn't mind an older man... All of you girls are so much younger, but would we really have loved each other?"

"Then came Halge," he continued, "and a dream revealed to me from the past that we had been deeply in love before... Well, she took the initiative, ignoring our age difference completely. That's what real love does, Hony."

Then, taking her hand, he said, "I don't know why I'm telling you all this. Perhaps to let you know that this old man also had his struggles. You're still young and now have Spirit as your companion. After having read the books, you know that you also can experience physical love. But, let's face it, today in this world of man with his terrible vanity — see it my way and do it my way — your future mate will have to be very special, with love in capital letters. The man who really loves you is very unselfish and only gets happiness out of your happiness." She was shaking her head...

He then followed it, "You think to find a man like that is utterly impossible. I know one thing, Hony, sitting here all day and going shopping once a week, going out with the girls on weekends, will not line you up with any man, period, certainly not with the right one. To have this beautiful friendship with the other girls has two sides to it, the love between you on one side — not very often found today — but the other side of the coin is, you do not get out on your own, where a man might come into your perimeter. You're not working, so go swimming every day, go dancing and attend other activities. Spirit will be of help, but you have to do your thing first. With your age, you'll see, you'll find the right man."

Getting up, he laughed, "And now you will have to drive me home. I got to get this jet lag out of my system."

A bit later at his house, she grinned, "You always seem to have the right answer and advice... When I find the right man, your wise words are needed

115

whether he is the right man."

Holding up his hands, he objected, "No, no, my dearest Hony, let Spirit do that job. I will not interfere."

After she had given him a kiss on the cheek, and before he had left the car, she simply said, "Sleep well, Andrew."

* * *

When Andrew showed up at Halge's place around noon the next day, he greeted her with the words, "I don't think I ever slept that long."

They embraced and she looked deeply into his eyes, whispering, "I'm still full of yesterday... We better not live apart, my lover, it's against our nature." And they kissed.

With the children at school, they sat down in the living room, where he asked with some anticipation, while holding one of her hands, "What did the children say?"

She grinned, "Louise in her innocence said that you're her dad already anyway, to her it's the most natural thing in the world. And Julia simply said that she loves you. Since she saw your mother's picture and discovered her likeness in looks, she feels very close to you. To Floyd it's not a question of having you as a father, but where to put you up rather. I think he needs a father most."

Looking at him for a reaction, she continued, "Your house is much larger than ours... You don't say anything, Andrew... What's occupying your computer up there?" She knocked on his head with a knuckle.

"It's all so fresh to me," he replied. "With us two all by ourselves it's so natural, as if centuries have col-

116

lapsed between us, our love is there on all levels of endeavor. How can we dress that in words. One feels it and my whole system is penetrated, if that is possible."

Then, still in deep thought, he continued, "Suddenly now the reality of fatherhood is upon me... It's not just to look after the children for a week, but for good, forever... I will have to handle their everything, not only with love, but also discipline, education, the whole spectrum of their growth. In my dreams I often thought about a situation like this, and now it's there, with a woman I love as I never did before. It's all presented to me on golden platters..." She grabbed him and their kiss was deep, the answer to their feelings.

After they had parted, she said with a grin, "I know one thing, my beloved, we have to learn to control ourselves in front of the children."

He nodded, patting her hand, "Yes, you're right, and that brings up the question again, do we want to live together? Sure, the children go to school and... It's all so new to me, Halge..." Then, "Let me experience the children when they come home from school. It'll simmer me down a bit. This guy needs help, and the children might just do the trick, if I may call it that, to level my consciousness."

* * *

The very first storming into the house was Floyd, and he asked, "Where is Andrew?"

His mother pretended not to know, so he walked from room to room and, coming back into the living room, he saw him — he had hidden behind the sofa.

Lifting him up, Andrew gave him a smirky grin

and said, "I thought I'd hide first and see what you'd do…"

"You are my dad now…" and he gave him a squeeze, again and again.

He obviously had run all the way from the bus stop, and when Louise entered the living room, she asked, "Are you our dad now, Andrew?"

"Well," he stalled with a deep grin, "your mother really wants me, and Floyd just told me that he wants me too. So, if I lift you up can you whisper it into my ear…"

On his arm, she said, "I don't want to whisper… You're my dad already for a long time and I love you too." She gave him a kiss, which made him blink.

Letting her down with a shaking head, he said, "With that kind of reception, maybe I should move in soon, what do you think, mother?" he grinned at Halge. Then, "We still have to see what Julia thinks…"

"She wants you too," was Louise's immediate interruption, "I know because she told me."

The school bus of the oldest one was an hour later, so the two rushed out to bring the news to their big sister. Shaking his head, Andrew commented, "I've never heard a bad word between them. Usually brothers and sisters fight each other."

"I've been blessed with all three of mine in that respect. Their love for each other is evident, no matter what they do."

When the three entered the house, Julia dropped her school books, came to Andrew and said, "Hi dad," and she put her arms around him, "I need a dad very much and as a dad I will kiss you," and she gave him a smacker. Then she said, "They say that girls should not kiss their fathers, but I will because I love you," and she gave him another smacker.

Giving his smirky grin, he replied, "I think this family does very very well. What do you think, mother?"

She grabbed him by the arm and whispered, "You still have any doubts, Dad?"

He gave her a quick kiss and barked, "No!"

At once Louise asked, "What did you whisper, Mom?"

She grinned, "Shall we tell them, Andrew?"

Looking from one to the other several times, he laughed, "Your mother asked me whether I still have any doubts. You see I wasn't too sure whether I would fit in and suggested letting you children do the choosing... And the rest is history, meaning I will try to be your dad from now on."

A moment later and before the children had gone to their rooms, Andrew suggested, "I very much would appreciate if you all continue calling me Andrew. I'm not your real dad... Well, we started off with Andrew, so we might as well stick with it. This family is different from all the families I ever knew, so we shall do this different too, if it's all right with you?" There was not the slightest argument about it.

After Julia had eaten an afternoon snack to satisfy her hunger before supper in the evening between six and seven, Andrew suggested, "I better change my eating times. Getting up at five, I have breakfast at five-thirty. Then my lunch is at eleven... It would be ridiculous that almost everyone in this house eats at a different time."

"Well, my dear ... husband — can I call you that already?" Halge asked grinning.

"Yes, you can, Mom," Floyd replied at once. "If he lives in our house, he is your husband."

Still grinning, Halge began again, "Well, my dear husband, most families with children, wives and husbands, often have no choice and eat at different times, but I wouldn't mind to have lunch with you together... How about twelve?"

Andrew nodded, then said, "Perhaps I was too rigid with my eating habits. Some changes have to take place in this man's life. How can there be any doubts?"

When the topic came up in which house they would live eventually, particularly the two small children aired their desire to stay where they were. The rooms in Andrew's house were too big for them.

Every day, the new family member moved some of his stuff over to the house of the Copperfields. However, he intended to keep his house for a while, there were simply too many things the smaller house was not roomy enough for. Then came the question of his beloved workshop...? So he suggested, "How about making a double garage out of yours. That should give me ample room to work on my gadgets and inventions."

The kids of the old neighborhood hated to see him go, and particularly Hollywood, his dog friend would miss him terribly. Who would take her out now? Although there were five kids in that family. And there was little Anna across the street with no father... The scooter would help her to overcome her loneliness.

* * *

With a lot of weekend hikes and bike rides, spring had come rather fast. Since the introduction of the scooter with the big wheels, at times it seemed to replace the bicycles. And very quickly Andrew's workshop also was discovered, where they could bring the two-wheelers for a quick repair.

"If we get married," Halge began the conversation one day, "I'll lose the thousand dollars a month. It doesn't make much difference to me. The marriage license is only a piece of paper, and we're very happy, license or not."

Andrew was thinking for a moment, then replied, "Let's consult my lawyer, whether there are any advantages. We certainly don't need the thousand bucks a month. What about the inheritance from Israel? I wonder how much it is and who was the one who wants you to have it to begin with?"

"Maybe I should show more interest in it," Halge mused. "We have been so happy in our togetherness, so what's a bit more money or not?" Halge took one of his hands and put it to her heart.

Halge had written a letter of inquiry to the lawyer in Jerusalem. Six days later, there was a telephone call from Israel, the very same lawyer was on the line, and he said, "You're in luck, Mrs. Copperfield. Without hearing from you, the money would've gone to a distant relative. I was wondering why you had so little interest."

Apparently, a great uncle of her husband, already over a hundred years old, had died and left his wealth — the amount of one hundred and eighty thousand dollars — to Leonard Copperfield in Canada. The money would now go to his wife, of course, since he was dead.

The lawyer said finally, "Please, Mrs. Copperfield, I would appreciate it if you would come here soon because your husband's brothers and sisters are on my back. They want the money and are willing to go to court. But it is specified in his will that none should go to them, for reasons I don't know. So you see, your letter came just in time and surely was appreciated by me. The sooner I can close this case, the better."

Andrew said, "We don't need the money, but I leave it to you..."

Halge replied, "Maybe we don't need it, but I want it... Perhaps now things even out a bit..." Then, "The way you look at me, Andrew, as if I wanted to get even. No, Leonard is dead and now I'm the rightful owner. How can I play with the thought of getting even?"

"Have you forgiven him, my beloved wife?" He looked at her, but her eyes did not hold his.

Then he said, "You have my support, Halge, besides, the kids will have their Easter holidays soon, so the time seems right."

Three days later, Andrew brought his wife to the Victoria airport and gave his last advice, "Do nothing without Spirit, and let it be your guiding light. Don't forget that in Israel, and particularly in Jerusalem, terrorists are still at work. Do nothing out of the ordinary. We want you back in one piece, Halge." They embraced and kissed.

* * *

Chapter 8

Israel

It was only a short flight to Vancouver, where Halge had to wait one and a half hours. It did not sit well with her to be on her own suddenly, so she bought a couple of books to keep herself occupied.

The next flight would be a very long one to Frankfurt in Germany. It actually was a relief to her when they finally lifted into the air, at least she was moving now toward her goal in Israel. She discovered some restlessness in herself and to overcome it she began to read.

The movie they were showing involved violence, so she tried not to watch it, but there was some classical music on her headset. They always seemed to offer something, food, drinks, bags with nuts, but her appetite was not very good because she could not really relax.

She began to think in terms, 'Perhaps I should've stayed home. I'm not used to this at all, but I want the money because it's rightfully mine.' Then she thought, 'I should have Andrew with me. We would comfort each other... His presence would make all the difference.'

The woman beside her tried several times to converse with her, but her English was hardly understandable. It surprised Halge how little German she still remembered from her early childhood. It was almost completely wiped out of her memory. This woman was on her way back to Germany. She apparently had visited her grandchildren in Canada, and now she was very satisfied with herself that she found them all healthy and OK.

'The language barrier is a terrible thing,' Halge thought. 'Will they understand me in Israel? As far as I've heard, they all speak English there.'

Almost everybody was asleep, but Halge couldn't in her upright position, no matter how hard she tried, besides, she wasn't tired at all. Then the thought crept up in her mind again, 'Maybe I should've stayed home. Andrew wouldn't have gone... So we can add a hundred and eighty thousand more dollars to our account. So what... We don't need it, as Andrew said.' She simply could not still her thoughts.

When Halge finally had fallen asleep, kind of, it was announced to get ready for the landing in Frankfurt. There were freezing temperatures, so she took a thick sweater out of her carry-on, although she would not leave the airport terminal. It would be a two hour wait for the next flight to Israel, but she intended to look around a bit.

To Halge's satisfaction, everybody spoke English and she found out very quickly that the terminal was of an enormous size. A friendly man, obviously an experienced air traveller, suggested to her to find her gate of departure and stay put because if she wanted to run around with her carry-on on wheels, she might get lost. "Your two hours of waiting fly by like nothing, and there you're ready to board the plane. Many people loose their flight connection, thinking they have plenty of time to look around."

Indeed, it was good advice because it took her more than half an hour to find her gate, and before she knew it, the boarding had begun.

The crew of the Israeli airplane and the attendants were very accommodating and very friendly. As the plane approached Israel, they contacted Halge's lawyer, so that he might've a car at the airport, for the drive to the hotel in Jerusalem.

It had become dark outside and not much could be seen through the windows. Over the Mediterranean Sea, the inside lights were dimmed and the shades over the windows secured, a simple procedure, not to give any terrorist any ideas, as a gentleman beside Halge explained. "Those people don't shy away from anything." he said. He prided himself to be an Israeli and knew what he was talking about.

Finally down at the Ben Gurion airport and pulling her carry-on to leave the terminal, Halge detected a man, holding up a sign with her name on it. As she approached him, he said, "I'm here for Mr. Hensel, your lawyer. If I could see your passport, please. I have to make sure that you're Mrs. Copperfield." Satisfied, he took her outside to a waiting limousine, to drive her to the hotel in Jerusalem.

"It's all paid for," he unloaded her at the hotel entrance, "I work for this hotel and if you need a car, let them know at the desk, please." He refused to be tipped.

As soon as she had entered her room, she felt very tired and went at once to bed.

Halge had hardly left her waking state, and she found herself in the mode of a dream, not that she knew to be in it herself. It was very much lifelike to her.

She was watching a fireworks display over the water at the horizon, together with other people, all looking out of the bus windows they were riding in. Everyone enjoyed the spectacle and even opened the windows to be able to see better.

Suddenly then, her attention was directed to the street below, on where they were riding slowly, and there fluttering in the wind was a lot of paper money. Halge held out her hand to catch some, but then thought that she didn't need it because she already had a hundred and eighty thousand dollars.

The next thing she experienced was that one of the firework rockets hit the bus and the people began to scream, many of them had been maimed... As she was looking down, she discovered that one of her legs was hanging sidewards. Then she discovered that blood was oozing out of her blouse and pants, but it was not painful. She thought, 'The fireworks could never have done that. It must've been a real rocket...' They all shouted, "It's a rocket attack. They want to kill us..."

Waking up out of this trauma of a dream, Halge could still hear the words, "They want to kill us..." Wide awake now and sitting up, she put on the night table lamp and thought bewildered, 'What was that?'

Out loud she said, "I dreamed... it was a dream!"

Her tiredness made her fall asleep again. This time it was dreamless.

When the telephone rang in the morning, it was Rudy Hensel, the lawyer, and he asked, "I wonder whether we can meet this afternoon?"

'Afternoon?' Halge wondered and asked out loud, "Can't I see you this morning?"

He replied, "It's already eleven and..."

"Eleven?" she called out... "I just woke up and could've sworn it was only eight."

He laughed, "Jetlag. Let me know when you're ready. How about at two? I'll be in my office then."

In the bathtub, Halge was thinking about the terrible dream and she wondered whether it had any significance or was it just a bad dream? And then, as she was drying herself, she thought, 'I'm going to ask the lawyer, he is bound to know whether the bus rides are safe. I wish I had Andrew with me right now. He's so good at this.'

She had a good meal in the hotel dining lounge. The food was excellent. She was joined by a woman from the States, who had been here several times before. She learned a lot from her, what were the different bus routes and how safe it would be. "For sightseeing go along the Mediterranean and stay away from the borders with the Arabian countries. If you're not a Jew or Christian, you have no interests in some of those sights, where people wind up dead. My husband, who is not a Jew and never comes with me, is always glad when I'm home again." And so she went on, explaining the different religious sights she was going to visit.

* * *

"Your husband's relatives are as different as day and night," the lawyer was telling Halge later on, "some are outright nasty and I'm sure glad to get this over with. So, let's do the signing and in a couple of days the money will be in your bank account, as you wanted it, Mrs. Copperfield. I don't even want to see your passport. I know an honest lady when I see one."

After she had signed the different documents, he said, "I guess you're on your way back home again soon. As long as you're here, I want to tell you something about the areas you better stay away from. Almost every week one of those fanatic Arabs blows himself up, and many of our people are killed, including children. As you were telling me, you're not interested in any of those religious sights anyway."

With some concern about her safety, Halge replied, "I was advised to take a bus tour along the Mediterranean Sea, and while I'm here, I wouldn't mind to see some of your country."

"Along there, you have nothing to fear. Take the evening bus because it's more beautiful." With that, he shook her hand and said, "Goodbye."

* * *

Back at the hotel, Halge inquired about the bus route and the time of departure. "Be outside the hotel entrance at seven thirty. The bus will be back at twelve o'clock. The driver will have your ticket, but you will have to show your passport, Mrs. Copperfield, or you won't get on."

Back in her room, she wondered whether to phone Andrew and the children. Time wise it would be very early for them, but at least I should let Andrew know that I have it all settled now and am more or less on my way back home again. Her flight was already booked for the next day at eleven in the morning and one only had to wait in Frankfurt for an hour.

She could hear the phone ringing and at once heard Andrew's voice, "Oh darling, we've been waiting for your call... Is everything all right?"

"I'll be back in two and a half days, my beloved husband, there's nothing to worry about." Then, "I guess the kids are still in bed?"

"Here comes Julia now, the ringing woke her up no doubt," Andrew replied.

"We miss you Mom," the oldest said, "come back home soon, please."

"I will, I will," was the happy reply. "Give a hug to your brother and sister for me."

After the short conversation, she felt very happy and thought, 'Compared with here, we're living in paradise on our island in Canada.'

* * *

It had begun to darken when Halge entered the bus with many other sightseers, and off they drove. There were many ships on the sea and their lights mirrored in the water. Apparently, as the bus driver explained over the speaker, there would be a pleasant surprise in store for them soon. It would be a fireworks display, coming from one of the Israeli military ships. "Lucky you," the bus driver was saying, "this display is only put on once a year in memory of one of Israel's gallant officers, who lost his life in our battle for freedom." Then, "For obvious reasons, the fireworks are kept a secret 'til the last moment. I just was informed about it by radio."

All the passengers displayed excitement, but Halge couldn't help harboring the thought, 'I wonder whether this has something to do with my dream? No, it couldn't be... If they kept it a secret until now. No, I better calm down. They're not stupid to let this happen.'

They might've driven for half an hour, and people already had taken their attention off the sea again, when suddenly, the fireworks spectacle had begun. It looked unbelievably beautiful because the sea water was mirroring the display. Some of the rockets went high into the air where they exploded and plunged into the water, still alight.

As the bus slowly moved along the highway, it came closer to the military ship, so that some of the rockets hit the water not too far away. Suddenly then, something hit the bus, and it was not coming from the fireworks display. It seemed to be a grenade from a rocket launcher. It did not explode right away, but when it did, it caused havoc in the truest sense of the word. The bus had rammed into a stone wall and stopped.

Halge could only hear screams and she wondered why she did not say anything because her lower body felt numb. There was no feeling left. Feeling with her hands down, one of her legs was not where it was supposed to have been. Coming up with her hands again, they felt slimy. 'It must be blood,' she thought. When she began to feel pain, it was so severe that she lost consciousness.

*　*　*

Halge did not know how much time had elapsed, when she noticed herself hovering above the theater of a surgery table, with white-clothed men working on a body. It was Halge's own body. After she had come to that realization, she zoomed back into her body, and again lost consciousness.

*　*　*

When the badly-wounded Halge came to, she saw the face of a man in white clothing above her, and he asked, "Can you year me, Mrs. Copperfield?" She nodded. "I have operated on you and we were able to save your right leg. You were speaking about Andrew and your children... What we could make out, you came to Israel for an inheritance and you said that Andrew never would've done it. I presume he is your husband?" She nodded vigorously and whispered, "I want to speak with him, he has to know..."

The man was the head surgeon and he spoke to the nurse behind him. Then he said, "We found your Canadian telephone number and we will arrange to speak to your husband by phone, but it's the middle of the night there. By the way, you have been out for over three days and your husband is probably wondering not having heard from you."

They had given Halge a small cell phone, and after only two rings, she could hear Andrew's voice. He knew it was her, and he asked excitedly, "What happened, my beloved wife? We worry very much about you... Are you there, Halge?"

With much joy in her voice, she answered, "Oh, Andrew, oh, Andrew, we were riding in a bus and a grenade hit us, but the doctor says that they could save my leg... I was out for over three days, darling.

This is the first time I can think again. Oh, I'm so weak, I hardly can speak. The doctor wants to speak with you..."

"I'm Dr. Houston," he took over the conversation. "Your wife is still very weak, Mr. Copperfield, but we think she's beginning to improve now. We could save her leg, but it'll probably need one or two more follow-up operations. If you have the means, there might be better surgeons in America, better qualified than we are here. It has to be seen."

Anxious to have his say, Andrew asked simply, "Will my coming there be of help?"

"Of course it will, Mr. Copperfield. While she was out, your wife spoke often of you and the children. How she wished she had not come here."

"Let me speak to her again, please. I will come as soon as possible."

With Halge on the phone, Andrew said, "Oh, my darling, we will get you through this ordeal. I'll pack at once and be on my way and will see you soon. Hony will be only too glad to look after the kids. Besides, Julia is a big girl already and a big help. So, don't you worry, I'm practically on my way and will see you soon. Think about Spirit. It will help us, I'm very sure of that. I love you, Halge. We all love you."

The phone was already disconnected and she whispered, "I love you too, I love you too, Louise, Floyd and Julia..."

* * *

With the children out of the bed and at the breakfast table, Andrew said, "By the way, I spoke with your mother during the night. No wonder we didn't hear from her because she was wounded in a rocket attack, but they operated on her leg and it seems OK now." Andrew tried not to make a big thing out of it and stay calm with his usual self, so as not to upset the children.

A bit later, and after everyone had eaten, he said, "I'm sure you'll all agree with me if I go to Israel myself to be of help to your mother and cheer her up. I think she needs my strong hand right now. After all, we want her back as soon as possible. Mind if Hony stays with you for a while?"

"We love her too," Louise said at once.

The children were remarkably calm, when he ushered them to the school bus. After he had phoned Hony first, he began to pack.

Hony came rushing into the house with her stuff in a couple of bags and said with disgust, "Those people down there are simply crazy... Rocket attack, hey?" She shook her head, then said, "Don't you guys worry about anything here. Just get Halge back in one piece." Their goodbye embrace was very strong and filled with love.

* * *

In Vancouver, Andrew phoned William Herding, the industrialist and his uncle, and he said, "William, I simply have to thank you for the fifty thousand dollars you placed in my bank account. I never thought I would use it, but now it will help us a lot. You see, my wife was badly wounded in Israel during a rocket attack and... Well, she might need one or two more operations..."

"Listen, Andrew," William interrupted him, "the little amount I gave you is nothing in comparison with what I got from you, my friend. I'm like new... I can walk again and no more wheelchair! I wanted to phone you and tell you, but never got around to it. Thanks to the spiritual aspects you opened up to me, and the beautiful life after death you introduced me to... I tell you, Andrew, my whole life is ... revolutionized, to say the least. We must meet and speak again... But first of all, we must attend to your wife's needs."

They talked for a long time, and William said finally, "Don't be shy and modest, Andrew, after all, we two are still alive from us old relatives and must stick together. What do I do with my billions? But now they can be of help to your wife! If she has to go to another place for a follow-up operation, I'll send a plane..."

Then William said once more, "From one relative to another, Andrew, please, give me the chance to help."

"Yes, William," Andrew couldn't help saying, "we must become good friends and stick together in today's world of violence. You will hear from me for sure."

* * *

When Halge saw Andrew come into the hospital room, she called out, "Oh, my beloved, you are here... Now all will be all right. Oh, to have you near me... I want your kiss, Andrew. I must feel it..." And their lips pressed together with tears running... Their hearts and souls expressed deep love for each other.

* * *

Chapter 9

Sophisticated Surgery

It's only good that they had the means now and asked for a private room so that Andrew could stay with Halge and even have his bed in there.

There was so much to tell. Andrew remarked, "In spite of the terrible happenings to you, we're fortunate that we can afford many things now many a poor person could not. And the offer of my uncle will give us the means to really find the best surgeon for you, my darling, no matter where he might be. We will get you on top of the world again."

A moment later, Halge asked, "I kind of wonder what lesson is in all of this. What karma are we ... or rather, what karma am I confronting? You have any idea?"

After some deep thinking, he replied, "It's not only you. It's all of us, we're not separated in solving this ... or dealing with this karma. Sure, if you would've taken the hint from the dream, if you're more familiar with dreams and their meaning, you probably would not have gone on that bus tour. You probably even would've gotten off the bus when the fireworks started. And the money on the street? Perhaps it was meant that it got you into this, meaning, if you wanted the money, you will have to suffer, although that also could've been avoided. Dreams like that should be heeded, and, to begin with, properly analyzed and interpreted. It's a vast subject, Halge, and we'll do well to study it more thoroughly in the future."

A moment later, he said once more, while holding one of her hands, "We're all put together again, you, the children and me — and in a lesser way perhaps, the five ladies also — to solve old karma. It's not just that we love each other, which all by itself is a wonderful thing, but all our passions and virtues will be played out. Time wise, we hardly met in this present life. Let's see what we have done to each other in ten or fifteen years from now. We're not living in paradise where everything works out smoothly. Let's see what'll happen when I have to apply some discipline to one or two of the children... And so I could venture into all kinds of happenings," he grinned, "but one thing is for sure, all of us are not put together to cater only to our deep love for each other."

Some time later, he said, "Of course, I don't want to belittle our present state of being, the love we have for each other is much, much more than most people display and feel, because it's the true love of heart and soul."

Halge pulled him over to herself and simply said, with tears in her eyes, "Kiss me, Andrew." It was the kiss of two souls.

* * *

136

In the afternoon they had a meeting with the head surgeon, which Andrew had requested. This time Dr. Houston entered without his white attire, and they shook hands again. After the doctor had inquired about Halge's well-being and how she was feeling, he said, "I have an idea what's occupying your minds. So, here I've brought a chart, not about your leg, but about your other two wounds, on your chest and your intestine, more correctly, your uterus. Both have healed remarkably well, but you will not be able to have more children, Mrs. Copperfield. Otherwise, there're no complications."

Andrew replied, "We're glad to hear that. My wife's leg is our big concern though. How much more surgery is required to put it into top shape again?"

Holding an X-ray against the light, the doctor explained, "It's hardly visible, but the main bone of your upper leg, has still a hairline break. In time it will heal without more surgery. However, as you can see, your knee bones, Mrs. Copperfield, are badly damaged. They could be replaced by a metal joint, as it is so often done today. As far as we know, there's only one surgeon who does some sophisticated surgery, and he might be able to save the bone. It is Professor Hoffmann in Berlin. But," he raised his eyebrows, "it does not come cheap, unless you're in the German health insurance, and even they're reluctant to pay, as we hear. So, you might want to opt for the metal knee."

Not hearing anything from either Halge or Andrew, he went on, "The metal joint does reasonably well, not that you could ever run again, to give one example. We could do all that here and our price is very reasonable. Think it over and let me know soon.

"Can we keep the X-ray?" Andrew asked.

"It's yours," Dr. Houston handed it over. "Talk it over." He raised a hand and left.

Halge began, "I don't know, Andrew ... Sophisticated surgery, which probably means I'm out again for days... If only I had..."

"Shhhht," he put a hand over her mouth, "we're living in the now, darling, never think of what you could've or should've done. Self-blame is a terrible drag, Halge, we have nothing to do with it. And now we will not touch the subject again until tomorrow. Good sleep or even a dream might give us the answer."

A bit later, he said, "In about two hours, Hony and the children will get up. How about being cheerful when we give them a ring, that everything is all right here. With the weekend coming up, we can have a long conversation with them and see what's going on at home."

After only one ring, Hony was on the line and said, "I had a feeling you would call, so I got up early. The children should be down any minute. They always seem to sense when you call. Here they come ... We're on the speaker."

"Hollywood came here yesterday," Louise called out, "and we had to bring her back. That she found us so far away..."

"She misses you, Andrew," Julia said, "they have to keep her on the leash now."

Halge said, "It's a wonder that she found her way there. But they have five children, and one can look

138

after her."

"We would," Floyd said immediately. "Hey, Mom, we all will help Hony with the wash tomorrow, and she didn't even ask us," he added.

Hony cut in, "The three are simply wonderful. And how are things there?"

"Well, I will have to have another operation to tidy things up kind of. The important thing is that I can walk again, and that I will! And now I will let you go, to get ready for school. Tomorrow we'll call an hour later because you're not in school then. So, think about something we can talk about. Goodbye, you four, we love you."

"We love you too," they all called back, "you and Andrew," Louise added quickly.

* * *

"I have a telephone call from Prague for you, Mr. Herden," a nurse had entered the room of Halge and Andrew. It was William Herding, and he said, "I've made up my mind, Andrew. I will come there with my plane, not only to help your wife, but also to meet her and you again, of course. What would be the best time?"

With some joy in his voice, Andrew replied, "I really look forward to that, William, but wouldn't it be better after Halge has her follow-up operation behind her?"

"My mind is made up, Andrew," was his rather stern reply, "I want to help when it's needed, and not later on. OK, when will it be best, Andrew?"

"Any time," he answered.

They agreed to meet the same day at eight pm at Andrew's hotel, where he still had his room. Andrew was waiting in the lobby, when William approached him. Their handshake was strong and neither one said anything for a moment, but looked into each other's unwavering eyes.

Grinning then, Andrew greeted the new/old visitor, saying with a thoughtful nod, "I'm facing a new William all right ... I don't even want to think back when I saw you last time..."

He gave him a smile, hooked into his arm, and said, "Neither do I want to warm up the old, but it was you, Andrew, who opened the spiritual window for me, and to think that my old religion was so terribly narrow, so..."

Raising his hand with his old smirky grin, he simply replied, "Whatever, William, we're living in the now!"

Smiling, his uncle couldn't help saying, "I was healed by Spirit."

Still smiling, he said a bit later, "Now we're brothers, Andrew, so let's act like brothers." If there was any kind of ice between the two, it was broken.

A hotel boy with some luggage was noticed by Andrew, so he suggested, "Perhaps you want to get to your room first, before I take you to my wife. I'll wait here."

"Yes, first things first ..." Fifteen minutes later, William joined Andrew again and said, "It won't be too late to visit her in the hospital?"

"We have a private room there, and come and go as we wish."

After the two had entered the hospital room, William greeted Halge, "May I call you also by your first name, Halge?"

She held out her hand and replied, "Please do, please do. With what I've heard of you, first names will do just fine," she grinned.

"You two are happy, I can see that," William said. "We much get you on your feet again... Too bad we just couldn't pull down Spirit to heal your leg."

"Spirit will help, William..." A nod was the reply.

After they had briefed William about Halge's leg and the possibilities available to bring it into good shape again, he asked, "What do you intend to do?"

"We'll know in the morning," was Andrew's simply reply.

William had opened his mouth already to follow it up, but closed it again. He suddenly realized that he would be out of order to suggest anything. The two obviously knew what they were doing. He thought to himself, 'I got to get this 'know it all' as a big shot industrialist out of my system. These two people are probably closer to Spirit than I am.'

Out of the 'blue', William said then, "The five virtues... You mentioned them, Andrew, when you visited me the first time. That we should adhere to them if we want to become the tool for Spirit. Would you please mention them again ... right now?"

Andrew had an idea what went through his uncle's head, so he said, grinning, "Beside the so-very-important Law of Love, there are Discrimination, Forgiveness-Tolerance, Contentment, Detachment — from material things — and Humility."

Nodding, William replied, "You've got me out of my life of ignorance and misery at one time, and it sure made a new man out of me. Often enough, however, the virtues still escape me. I need a reminder..."

Andrew laughed, "You're not the only one. How often are we pestered by vanity, anger and what have you. The thing is though, to recognize it and stop it outright. I read once that this woman had the virtues and passions stamped on a metal plate, then hung it around her neck, to be always reminded. It might be an idea..." he grinned.

Grinning with him, Halge said then, "I don't need a metal tag around my neck. I have this man. He knows the virtues by heart." She looked at him with love.

Andrew, taking one of her hands, then said, "No, my beloved wife, it's the other way around." Their look at each other said the rest.

Getting up, William said, "I envy you two. When will we see you tomorrow?"

Andrew explained, "In the morning we'll have a long conversation with the children back home. How about in the afternoon at two? After our stomachs have been filled."

"I shall be back," with that William left.

* * *

Halge had the following dream: She found herself running with her oldest daughter, Julia, several times around the block, always saying, "let's do it once more. I want to do it ten times." Then she was breathing hard, hanging onto a tree, so as not to fall over. End of dream.

In the morning, she remembered it so vividly, that she had not the slightest trouble passing it onto Andrew. With a deep smile he asked, "And the meaning of it is?"

She thought for a moment, then said, "I'm going

to get that operation done in Berlin. I'm still not wholeheartedly into it. I don't want to be out for three days. It scares me. What if I don't wake up again?"

However, after they had consulted Dr. Houston, the head surgeon, later on, he put her worries to rest by saying, "At times they only put the lower part of your body to sleep, so that you are fully aware of the goings on. I don't know how Professor Hoffmann does it, but I can assure you, you will not be out for three days. I predict that in twenty-four hours you'll be awake again. The pain of the operation has to be subdued, of course, for a few days. Now I will tell you, Mrs. Copperfield, I personally would've decided on the same operation. If one has the means... Your leg will almost be like new again."

*   *   *

Fortunately, they were able to get a speaker phone, and now Andrew was dialing their home number. After the first ring, Hony answered, "Hi you two! We're all here and have a lot to tell and to ask. Louise is first."

"How did you know it was us?" Halge asked.

"Who else would phone us, Mom?" Louise answered. "Hi Mom, hi Andrew. Our bus didn't go one day, so Hony had to drive us to school, but not Julia. There was a new teacher and he has two children. Now they're our friends."

Then Floyd spoke, "They're our age, a boy and a girl. And Hony likes the teacher too, he visits us."

Hony laughed, "Things are revealed very quickly, ha ha. Well, the new teacher, Fred Sounders, and his two children, happen to live nearby. He's a widower and just moved here two weeks ago from the east. In any case, when I brought the two to school, we got to talk and found out we were not living too far apart. It was mainly his children, just having lost their mother, to have found a liking to Louise and Floyd. So, here they are with new friends, and the father dropped in too, to find out whether his children were safe. We had a tea then, that's all."

"Hi Mom and Andrew," Julia was anxious to have her say, "now it's my turn. I was selected for the track and field team because I'm the fastest runner, faster than most of the boys."

"I'm not surprised," Halge cut in, "you always were good on your legs, Juli. When I come home, which will be soon, you have to take me running around the block, so that my leg will get in good shape again."

"By the way," Andrew said quickly, "tomorrow, which is a Monday, we'll fly to Berlin because there is a professor who will do some sophisticated surgery on your mother's leg. We'll bring the X-ray, so you will be able to see how your mother's leg was before the operation."

Then Halge said, "Aren't we lucky to have Hony to help out and do all the work."

"We also help," Louise said at once.

"Yes, my little one," Halge said, "what would we do without you?"

"Floyd helps too," Louise said quickly.

"And so does Julie," Hony added.

"I sure like my new friend," Floyd said, "and he likes my scooter. Louise lets him drive hers, so we can go together."

Then Hony said, "I think it all was said now. Will you call from Berlin as soon as possible?"

"Of course," Andrew replied, "of course."

Halge added, "We love you all!"

"We love you too," it came as if out of one mouth.

* * *

"We decided to go to Berlin," they greeted William Herding.

He said at once, "Let's go then, my plane is at the Ben Gurion Airport."

After a few moments of thought, Andrew said, "We have to do some packing and finish it off here. We also have to pay our bills..."

Interrupting him, his uncle said, "That can be done later..."

Taking his arm, Andrew asked rather puzzled, "Why do you want to rush us, suddenly, William?"

"Well... I mean... Of course you're right. It's the businessman in me and my age ... I cannot get used to the fact that I still might be around for a year or two."

"Or five or even ten years, William," Andrew patted his arm.

Smiling and inhaling deeply, he answered, "I'll go down and pay for everything, and that you will not prevent." Then, "I'll be back in two hours."

* * *

The Israeli physician had left a message on the professor's phone in Berlin and sent a fax at the same time because it was a Sunday and nobody was answering.

After their landing in the capital city of Germany, it was dark already, but William had arranged for an

145

ambulance to take them to the nearest hospital. He was the master of the physical world and everything was looked after. Watching him, Andrew realized that it would have been useless to say anything. His uncle had only one thing on his mind, and that was to help, the help of an industrialist with a strong mind.

*　*　*

When Professor Hoffmann appeared at the hospital the next morning, he was all 'business', meaning he wanted to go to work as soon as possible.

After he had examined Halge's leg and particularly her knee, he said in fluent English, "I shall take another X-ray, but I would like you to come to my hospital where I have all my own equipment. I'm sure that we can go ahead in the morning. As I have been informed, financially everything is taken care of."

Andrew asked, "How long will the operation take? Will you be so kind and keep us informed about everything? And can I stay with my wife at your hospital?"

"That can be arranged," the bearded man of fifty or so answered, while stroking his beloved goatee. Besides being a top-notch surgeon, he obviously also liked to increase his funds.

Having another look at the X-ray, he said, "Without complications, the operation will not take longer than six hours. So, if you come to my hospital today, we will do the operation in the morning at seven."

Andrew asked, "Would you be so kind and send one of your own ambulances, please?"

He nodded and replied, "It should be here within the hour." He left without another word.

Inside the new hospital, it was much more elaborate. Obviously, it was a place for the rich with a lot of money. Andrew had an idea that his uncle had worked behind the scenes and let them know that nothing should be spared... It chilled him, kind of, that he had no control over these goings-on. The other side of the coin was, however, that Spirit had arranged this perhaps, since they might've had a hard time to pay for this operation, whatever the cost might be. He couldn't quiet his thoughts, 'Or, with over two hundred thousand in our account... It could've been enough. Perhaps I'm unjust, but something is against my grain.'

*   *   *

When Halge was brought back into their hospital room, after a five-hour operation, she still was in a deep sleep, and the attending nurse said, "The professor will see you in the late afternoon, then your wife should be awake again. Please do not give her any food. She can have some juice, which I will bring you. If you need any help, ring the bell, please." She pointed to the button on the wall and left. She too spoke very good English.

Stroking his wife's forehead, Andrew said quietly, "In a month or two, darling, you will be on your leg again, and it will be in the presence of our beloved children."

The first who appeared in the afternoon was William, and he asked, "How is she? The professor tells me that the operation was a complete success. Well, he will tell you that himself. I'm here to say goodbye. Since Halge is still not awake, you will give her my regards, Andrew. I have an idea what you're thinking about me... Well, if I live long enough, I still might be able to adopt all the virtues. Forgive me please if I appeared too harsh at times. The old industrialist is coming through. It's difficult to shake."

Then, trying to smile, "In any case, if I put everything on a scale, on one side the revelations of Spirit and karma, the things you gave me, including getting this old body out of the wheelchair again, and on the other side the things I could give you, which was only money of which I have plenty, your side of the scale goes way down. By the way, everything is paid for, including your airfare. Take the hundred and eighty thousand home, and be happy with it. You two deserve it."

After a strong handshake, he left, and Andrew would never see him again. Shortly after, he died of heart failure. However, the last reminder of William Herding was a beautiful bouquet of twelve red roses, brought in by the nurse soon after he had left.

Halge had been awake for half an hour, and the two mostly smiled at each other, with a few words of love in between, when Professor Hoffmann entered the room. Nodding, he said, "You're doing fine, my dear. We did a splendid job, as we usually do. The operation was very successful. I must warn you, though, not to use your leg for a while, and then walk only with two crutches. I'll give you a letter for your doctor at home."

Then he said with a grin, "It's good to have a benefactor, as you have, this Mr. Herding from Prague. How did you get to know him, if I may ask?"

Andrew couldn't help grinning back, "You mean Uncle Herding ..."

"He is your uncle?" the professor burst out, "I

didn't know."

With his smirky grin this time, Andrew replied, "Only a year ago I didn't know him either."

*　*　*

Chapter 10

Home Again

Halge had to get up in the middle of the night and sitting up, she realized how difficult it would be to do it on her own, so she threw a pillow at Andrew who woke up immediately. As he sat up, he said, "I see you need my help. Don't try to do that on your own, darling, as long as I'm here. I'd hate to see you falling to the ground," he gave her a light slap on the back.

Later she said, "I'm not tired anymore…"

He replied, "Then we shall have a little night wrap, meaning I shall snuggle up beside you," he grinned, "and you will tell me what you're thinking."

To his surprise she said, "I was born in Germany, but hardly remember the language, although I was already thirteen when I left. I wonder why?"

Thinking for a moment, he suggested, "When we have experienced something very negative in the past, we tend to wipe it out of our mind. That might be the case with you. Our mind with it's subconscious part is something like a complicated computer. That's why we have psychologists and psychiatrists to get rid of some mental blocks or whatever. Often by going back to the place where it happened will solve the problem."

"I kind of wonder," she reflected, "whether being back in my birth country has anything to do with my desire to visit this city by driving around and seeing the historical sights. At one time I wanted to escape from my painful past — not that I remember what it was — but now... Well, I wouldn't mind seeing more of it again."

He laughed, "Perhaps you were born in Berlin...?"

"No," she replied, "that I know. I was born in the west on the River Mosel in a little town. They made a lot of wine there. From there I slipped into France, where I worked for a while. I remember more of that language today."

"All right, my beloved wife, how about getting a comfortable car, where you can lie down and visit some of the sights. We'll inquire in the morning."

When they spoke to the nurse about it after breakfast, she said, "Our hospital has a special car for such cases. As long as you're with us, I will see that you can use it every day, if you wish. One of our nurses will be with you during those drives."

Andrew suggested, "How about on afternoons, and please see that her English is reasonably good."

The driver sure knew Berlin well, and he drove them to all the historical sights, including the former Berlin Wall, what was left of it. Fritz, the driver, was a very happy and often joking fellow, the way he presented everything. Often he had them laughing. That's what Halge needed and Andrew enjoyed tremendously. It too was his nature.

When Halge mentioned Frederick the Great, she had touched Fritz's favorite subject, and he suggested, "If Germany had had 'den Alten Fritz', the Old Fritz, instead of Hitler, the world would look different today. He never would've made war with France and England, and he sure would've dealt differently with Stalin and Russia. That man was way ahead of his time. To give one example: When France began to prosecute and condemn the Huguenots, he opened his arms and invited them into Germany, where religion was free. Today, you still find French names here in the northern part of Germany, but they don't speak French anymore."

And so Fritz went on ... Then Andrew interrupted him with the question, "Can we visit the place where he lived?"

"Potsdam," Fritz called out, "if we go there, we will have to make it a day and take something to eat. There's a lot to see."

So they prepared to drive to Potsdam the next day, and the hospital gave them a basket with all kinds of food, mostly sandwiches and several kinds of fruit, but also mineral water to drink.

When they entered Potsdam, Fritz showed his pride, this obviously was his most beloved city. "I was born here, so know all about Frederick the Great. And now I shall introduce you to the beautiful palace, Sans Souci ..., it means without worry."

Then, "He loved to speak French and spoke it most of the time."

Indeed, it was a place, a palace to behold! "But," Andrew began, "but from where did he get the funds to build this huge place? I mean, even in his time it must've been worth millions."

Fritz replied, "But he won almost all his wars... He only lost two, and they only... Well, he didn't get the land he wanted."

Andrew questioned, "You mean to tell me that the wars he won made him rich? That he could afford this... He didn't tax the people, or?"

Fritz explained, "All the good things he did..."

Suddenly feeling bad for what he had suggested, he interrupted him with a smile and said, "I was stupid to bring it up in the first place. Obviously Frederick the Great was a great man, for his time he certainly was. One always can find something negative in any deed and achievement."

When Fritz wanted to say more of his idol, Andrew simply said, "No, no, my friend, we're here to enjoy the sight of Sans Souci, and that's what we're going to do." Then, "Obviously, the king had many good things up his sleeve, or he would not have been so tolerant toward other religions, condemned in another country. The world can learn from that."

The nurse who had been quiet so far, said in her limited English, "All Germans loved the king. He was very popular." Then, "Hitler savored him because he was a great strategist to win his wars. That's how Hitler saw himself when he made war against the whole world. We like him today because he reminds us of what could've been, if Hitler had had his qualities, instead he made a mess out of Germany and Europe."

Fritz had parked the car, turned around and said, "You said that very well, Klara. I already was wondering what else I could've said to our visitors."

Andrew already wished he hadn't said what he did about Frederick the II, although there was a lot of truth in it. Obviously, these two German people didn't want to hear anything negative about their historical idol, still very popular today.

There was much more to be seen in Potsdam, of course, all very rich in the history of Germany. The beauty of the city and particularly the surroundings with the lakes, was very revealing to the visitors. Fritz went out of his way to explain it all, and he said once more, "There simply is not enough time to see the close and important environment also. We need days for that. All in all, that is Berlin and Potsdam and their surroundings could be a state or province on its own. Even we people pride ourselves to be different from the rest of Germany, ha ha." He wanted to give the impression that he didn't mean it, but one could feel that he did.

Back at the hospital and in their room again, Halge stated, "They say that Hitler was able to unite all the German people with their diversity and different dialects which made them so dangerous under his reign."

Andrew laughed, "It's still one country today, but not dangerous."

*   *   *

After three weeks and many telephone conversations with the children and Hony, the couple were told by the professor that the knee had healed enough to fly home again, because Halge had reached a point where she didn't need anymore pain killers.

So it was goodbye to the friendly hospital staff

and particularly to Fritz, the driver. One day he had surprised them with a book about Frederick the Great, written in English, and he refused flatly any pay. He said, "I've learned a lot from you too. I never before drove such a happy couple around, who really appreciated what I said and explained." And they shook hands.

With two crutches Halge was able to walk on her own and enter the plane for the long flight to England first and then home again.

Although it was in the middle of the week, Hony was at the Victoria airport with the three children, and she explained, with tears running down her cheeks, "There was no way I could've sent the three to school. It would've been too cruel... How do you control their love..."

Indeed, their hugging, mixed with tears was endless... Their hearts and souls expressed their love, impossible to dress in words.

After everybody had calmed down again, and after they had entered Hony's van with her at the wheel, Halge said, "By the way, Andrew and I have decided to get married..."

"But you're married already," Louise called out.

Grinning, Andrew took one of her hands, and replied, "Yes, you're right, of course, but we just want to make it official, meaning, they're putting it on a document, which we might want to frame and put on the wall, ha ha."

Hony laughed, "I'd like to see that..." Then, "Can I be the best man as a woman?"

"Do we want Hony as our best man, Halge?" Andrew asked with his old smirky grin.

"The answer to that shall remain unanswered because it would be frivolous." Then she explained to the children what a best man stood for.

A bit later, Halge said with a grin, "I remember driving down this highway and telling a certain man — you see I had picked him up from the airport instead of Hony — that I would like to see more of him in the future because I loved him very much."

"You said that to Andrew, I bet," Floyd burst out, "and now you're married already. When I'm old enough, I hope a girl tells me that too."

Andrew reached over to pat his arm, "Never be in any rush, Floyd, and never get married without love."

* * *

It took a few days to get settled in again and it also came to bear that the children's friends and their father had moved again to another house farther away.

When the adults were on their own, Hony was telling them that the teacher who had taken so much interest in her was not quite what she'd expected and she wished he would take her hint and not come for visits anymore with her back now again in her own home.

A few days later this came to a head, when Hony phoned Hety — living closest to her — and said crying and very upset, "He tried to rape me. First he began to undress me, over my loud protests, then he threw me on the couch to do his business. My screaming made him finally realize that I wanted no part in it, and he stormed out of my house."

"Calm down, Hony, I'll see you in a minute," Hety

replied. Her friend was terribly upset and said, "An educated man like him... I never gave him any lead that I wanted to go to bed with him. He gave me no chance to tell him that nor that I'm a bi-sexual. That man is crazy..."

All this made the rounds, of course, and Andrew remarked, "And a man like that has two lovely children... Poor Hony, she needs a mate more than any of us, but where does she find a man with her handicap?"

A moment later then, he followed it with the words, "Being so close to her, we feel very bad, and without her past life's history, we don't know what Spirit with her karma has in store for her."

"We will give her our love," Halge said, "and she knows that. We all stand by her. She knows that too."

Halge and Andrew had decided to adopt the name of Herden for the children also. "Copperfield for me and the children always leaves a bad taste. I want to get rid of it, and using both our names, Herden-Copperfield, is too much of a mouthful. I have no love for this double-name business, as seen so often."

When the adults brought it before the three children, Julia, the oldest one commented, "Copperfield is a Jewish name. Half of us kids' blood is Jewish, but I feel so much closer to Andrew today and his name is Herden. That's the name I want to grow up with." It made the most sense. And Floyd and Louise agreed by saying, "Me too," and "Me too."

It was decided not to make too much out of the wedding without any kind of celebration. "We're just getting it down on paper in front of the Justice of the Peace, observed by our two best men, Hony and Hety," Andrew suggested. "Then we'll send out some cards so that everybody knows what our name is now."

However, they didn't count on the five ladies, who surprised them with a big pizza party. Hety said, "We all have been married before, and will not let you get away with this because we know how important a love relationship is, and that's what you two symbolize to us."

It had Halge in tears and she said, "Oh, you girls, to have friends like you with your love..."

During the happy pizza wedding celebration, it also came to light that a certain teacher had taken his two children to move away again, which was a great relief to Hony.

Everybody was smiling, so Andrew thought it was a good occasion to say something which was on his heart for quite some time. He stood up and looked around with his old grin, then began, "You ladies know each other much longer than I know you. As a man, I kind of invaded your circle of friendship, and it so happened, I'm still the only man. Well, I don't know whether I should bring this up, but I do it anyway because for many years I was on my own, not that I was exactly happy with my situation. At one time I gave Hony a sermon about this already, and she probably knows what I'm getting at."

Not saying anything for the moment, Getta simply said, "If you're trying to get us a husband, I'm very happy on my own."

Hety said at once, "Let him speak, Getta, I, for one, don't mind to hear it."

Grinning, Andrew continued, "Of course, you're all different in what you want, but if you feel as I did for many years, you do feel lonely at times, if not all the time. Well, as old age was creeping up on me, it did not improve, on the contrary... Perhaps you might be able to figure that out for yourself. And when my wife of today came along with love for this old guy, something I almost had stopped dreaming about, I was the happiest man in the world. And on top of it, she brought along three beautiful children, ready-made, kind of... What can I say, but that suddenly a dream had become reality."

Halge had pulled him down to give him a kiss with blinking eyes, everybody knew the meaning of it.

A moment later, "So why did I open my big mouth? And what was it I wanted to say to begin with? Yes, Hony, you know because I talked to you about it before. However, you're not a working woman as the others are. At one time I told Hony to go out into life more than she does. Go swimming, dancing and what have you. Your friendship of love is unique, and you don't know what it did to me when you accepted me into your circle at one time. Yes, it made me very happy. This old guy who never had any luck with the opposite sex, suddenly found himself in the middle of five ladies, and what was the main ingredient? It was love in capital letters. Oh, I'm veering off again."

"It sounds very good though," Angela commented.

Laughing, Andrew continued, "But every good thing also has its opposite, and that's what I wanted to say. So, I will put the question to you. What can you guys do to attract good men into your orbit of love? I use the word orbit because it suggests, to me anyway, something noble."

The first one who spoke was Mira, and she said rather seriously, "You don't know how often I was thinking about the very same, and you tabled it, Andrew. I might not feel as lonely as you did at one time, but I don't intend to stay single for the rest of my life. Sure, we have each other, and often enough are very happy together, but it doesn't get us a mate, a man we can love. I'm glad it's in the open. So what can we do about it?"

With the exception of Getta, who was happy to be on her own now, they didn't mind to do something about it, but what?

When Hety mentioned to put an ad in a paper or magazine, it was discussed for some time, until Andrew suggested, "Why don't you let it sink in for a few days. You know very well, once it's put into the air, meaning Spirit has taken hold of it, a dream might give you the answer, as it was in the case with Halge's operation." And he explained.

Then he said, "I once read that every physical problem has a spiritual solution. But you have to do your part first. It will not work by just putting your hands into your lap and saying a prayer. We cannot manipulate Spirit or God even. It knows everything about us."

Louise said suddenly — and it made them all aware that the children also were present and listening in — "We'll help you to find a husband like Andrew." It sure took the seriousness out of their discussion.

Halge squeezed her little one, then said, "Yes, indeed, we all will help.

* * *

While in Israel and Berlin, Andrew had missed

his hikes, bike rides and swimming, but now had started it on a regular basis again. Halge was not up to anything of this nature, but Hony joined him, particularly when it came to swimming, because that exercise invigorated her.

One day, while leaving the Cowichan Centre, where the pool was located, he was approached by a younger man he had often seen in the hot pool. He said, "At times I see you with a young lady. I guess you're good friends...?"

Grinning, Andrew replied, "Yes, we're very good friends. In fact, Hony looked after our children while we were abroad. Why, do you have an eye on her?" he laughed.

The man continued, "By the way, my name is Robert. At the pool we only go by first names and I heard them calling you Andrew."

They shook hands. Then he said, "To tell you the truth, I'm very much interested in the lady. Did you say Hony was her name?"

Having a good look at the man, Andrew said with his old grin, "Yes, it's Hony without the 'e'. We're a close-knit bunch of people in Mill Bay, of which I'm the only man. It's a long story how we discovered each other, but I married one of the ladies, all much younger than myself, about your age I'd say."

Then, "I presume you would like to be introduced to my friend?"

"If you don't mind ... Better perhaps before we enter the pool." Andrew agreed.

Then he explained, "Hony does her wash today, or she probably would be with me. After swimming, we always hike from here. How about tomorrow in front of the ticket desk, where people gather and wait for each other?"

Robert replied, "I could be there at twelve, if that's OK with you?"

"We'll make it OK," Andrew laughed, and they parted.

On his long hike, Andrew thought, 'He looks like a decent man and I have a good feeling about him. Oh, I hope he will be the right one for Hony. Of all the others, she is perhaps the most lonely. But, being a bi-sexual ... He has to be a very special man.'

*   *   *

It was a day later, and Hony was very excited after Andrew had told her about his meeting with Robert. Before they drove off in their own individual cars, she said, "My heart is pounding, Andrew... He might've seen me several times before, but with you in my presence, he never had the courage. Is that a good sign, Andrew?"

He nodded, "I think it is." And they entered their cars.

Hony was hanging onto Andrew's arm, while he introduced the two. Then he said, "I'll see you in the pool then..."

However, Robert and Hony never came for a swim, and Andrew thought, 'Perhaps the two really hit it off right...'

After his water exercise and coming back to his car some time later, he found a note behind one of his windshield wipers, and it read, "We went for a hike along the old Cowichan railroad track road. We might see you there. Hony."

Grinning to himself, Andrew thought, 'I think I'll

do my hike along there too today and see whether I meet them. As nosy as I am, I want to see how the two are doing.'

It took him almost an hour before he discovered them on a turn-off, deeply involved in a discussion... When Hony noticed him approaching, she waved at him to join them.

Overjoyed, she greeted him with the words, "You'll never belief this, Andrew, Robert also has the very same spiritual beliefs we have. In fact he traveled all over the world to study under the different gurus... Boy, does he know the subject..."

Robert smiled, "As I hear, you have become their guru and introduced them to the law of karma and Spirit, and the way It will help us, if we believe in It's existence."

Andrew replied, "Indeed ... indeed, but I'm not their guru, young man. I just introduced them." Then, "And, now I will be on my way again because I need the workout, that is, my body needs it, while you two need a workout of a different nature," he grinned.

Hony slapped him on the arm, and grinned back, "Oh, you..."

The young couple might've seen each other for three weeks, when they invited everybody for an engagement party at Hony's house, which was a big surprise, but not so much to Andrew. He had had a feeling about it.

As all the girls and children entered the house with much excitement, it was an endless hugging with tears. As soon as Andrew had put his arms around Hony to give his best wishes, she whispered into his ear, "It's going to be all right… Everything, Andrew, everything." He knew, of course, what she was getting at.

There was no doubt about it, Hony and Robert loved each other. It was the real McCoy, everybody could see that.

At one point, Louise said, "Now we have to get somebody else to look after us, when Mom and Andrew are away."

Halge followed it with the words, "In June Julia will be thirteen, and she's very much responsible and grown already. So she will be quite capable to be your babysitter, my little one."

Nodding, Andrew agreed, "Yes, she's almost grown now. Besides, we will not go anywhere again, but rather put our attention on the betterment of your mother's knee. When you three are in school, we probably will begin with the riding of our bikes together."

Hony said then, "That probably will be without us because we'll make our home in Duncan. And for the time being, there're many things on our minds besides swimming, hiking and bike riding. Robert will have his own business, and he needs my help in that respect. In a year or so, we want to get back to exercising, of course, but it has to be in the evenings."

Andrew laughed, "Two gone, three to go." They knew what he meant and it made everybody laugh.

"What does that mean?" Louise whispered to her mother. So she explained to her little one.

When Hony put her house on the market before her move, Andrew suggested to Halge, "Perhaps I should sell my place also. Renting it out…? It might mean trouble. What do you think, my beloved? It's yours as much as mine."

"Let's sleep on it," she proposed with a grin, knowing that it always had been his idea to get an answer to a question.

*　*　*

Chapter 11

"Fiddle, Faddle...

Coming home from a swim and sitting in the hot pool at the Cowichan Community Centre in Duncan, Halge told Andrew, "This swimming and the hot water do me a lot of good, too bad we have to drive into town all the time. And, unfortunately, I can't accompany you on your long hikes as yet. So, you've got to drive me home, and I keep you away from your favorite walks around Duncan and north of it. We should have two cars, my husband."

Scratching his head, he replied, "Perhaps you're right, but two cars...? We should have a van though. With all of us in the car it's kind of crowded."

A few moments later, while they had an afternoon tea, and before the children would be back from school, she said, "Watching you now, my beloved husband, tells me that your mind is still working on what we've discussed... Are you going to let me in on what's occupying you up here?" she pointed to her head.

"Ha ha," he laughed, "it shows, doesn't it? Well, I

was computing and computing and I bet Spirit helped to come up with a suggestion, and that's all it is, a suggestion."

After a few more sips, he asked, "What would you say if we had our own swimming pool? Not just a hot tub, which many people have already in their back yard, but a real swimming pool, indoors with warm water during the winter? I can do much of the work myself. Not digging the big hole and the cement, but all the other installations, including the addition to the house with a solid roof. Of course, half of the garden will disappear... I don't know the particulars as yet, but I could begin with a drawing for all of us to see to have some input from everyone... What do you say, my beloved wife?"

Thinking and nodding, and thinking and nodding, Halge began, "Boy oh boy, our own pool... We then could go for a swim in the middle of the night... The kids sure would like that. Oh, Andrew, what an idea. But, let's not tell the children yet. You make a drawing first, then I make a picture of it, as it would look in reality. I'm not too bad with painting and the brush."

To the lady of the house it was not a case of accepting the idea of a pool, she already saw the finished product and dreamt of what they could do then. So Andrew did not bring up the fact that it would take a big chunk out of their bank account. For now they had his sizeable monthly income, and by the time he would leave his earthly home for good, there would be enough for Halge to live for the rest of her life. In any case, his thoughts did not linger for too long on it because the pool was important now and he would build it.

The parents decided to fill in Julia, after all, she was old enough to add some good ideas to the project. When they revealed it to her the same evening, after the two young ones had been put to bed, she was overjoyed, and her reaction was almost identical to that of her mother, dreaming of all the things they were able to do then, at home in their own pool.

*　*　*

It had become a daily routine during the week for the adults to drive for a swim into town because the therapeutic value for Halge's knee was too good to be ignored. She already was able to ride short distances with the bike, feeling better every day.

When the five rode together on weekends, Andrew had a seat for Louise on his bike installed. She was still too small to ride on her own and keep up with them. With Mira, Getta, Angela and Hety joining them at times, they had a lot of laughs, as if a big family.

With them all together at one time on their bikes, they encountered an elk with huge antlers, and it came right at them. As everybody was dismounting in a hurry, Andrew called out, "Hide behind the trees and be very quiet!" It still was the rutting season and this kind of elk was known to attack anything moving and in sight. They had no choice but to wait it out, hoping it would not damage the bikes. It finally lost interest and trotted off.

Before they were on their way again, Andrew said, "I don't mind a bear, they always run off anyway, but this huge elk...? I think I'm going to get a stun-gun, just in case... There're not always trees to hide behind."

"What about cougars?" Getta asked.

"I never even have seen one, and with us big bunch of people together, I don't think they'll come near us," Andrew explained.

*   *   *

Not too long hence, Andrew suggested, "We might as well get my house ready to be sold soon. Finally then I will be able to transfer the electric shoe cleaner to our porch here. We have been so busy that I never got around to it." He drove several times back and forth to bring all his stuff over he hated to part with.

From Andrew's drawing of the pool, Halge had painted a beautiful picture, as it would look in reality, attached to the main house. They also had added a storage building and 'his' and 'hers' dressing rooms, because sooner or later, visitors would come and they had to be catered to.

When the picture of the pool was presented to Floyd and Louise with Halge's explanation, the two were overwhelmed that they would have this in their own house soon. Many questions had to be answered... Could they bring their school friends over? Andrew said finally, "Our pool is not for the public, you guys. With the children, parents also will come because adults have to be present. There always is the danger of drowning. How do we know they're good swimmers? It's not that you just play with your friends in the water as you do in the garden or on the street. An experienced adult has to be present, as the lifeguards are at the Duncan pool. You've seen them."

Then Halge added, "I think we will have to teach

169

you children the real meaning of discrimination. The meaning of it is most of the time not understood. It means to be able to judge properly. Why don't you ask your teacher to explain it to you. Andrew and I are great believers in it, because it is a very important virtue, perhaps equal to love, forgiveness and humility. Well, I kind of got side-tracked, but there is a serious side to having a swimming pool, and you have to respect it."

Then Julia asked her siblings, "You know who painted this beautiful picture? It was Mom! Isn't she a great artist?"

Putting an arm around his wife, Andrew agreed, "So she is. I wouldn't mind to see that kind of picture on one of our walls. Look at all the pictures I've brought from my house, while you haven't got a single one in the living room."

With some seriousness in her voice, Halge stated, "To go into that means to warm up the past, and..."

"Don't say anything," Andrew interrupted her, "it was stupid of me to say what I said. We'll begin with the now, and this beautiful picture of yours will be the first... Where shall we hang it?"

At once Halge replied, "I will do a larger one and we will put it up opposite the large window over the sofa. Do you all agree?"

"Can I have the small one in my bedroom?" Louise asked immediately.

"After we've framed it, it's yours, little one," Halge gave her a squeeze.

Later that evening, when the two adults were on their own, Andrew suggested, "I have an idea how to have warm water all the time in our pools, particularly the hot pool. We shall heat it with the power of the sun. Unfortunately, Mill Bay is in the shadow of the Malahat Mountain located, so we do not get the benefit of the sun all the time. However, if we do it right, it should be enough for our pools, without using the expensive electricity."

* * *

The hired architect had made a proper drawing, so that it all would be legal with the local authorities. There would be a water reservoir under the pool to store the water, heated by the solar panels, which meant a lot of earth had to be gotten rid of and hauled away.

Andrew's house had been sold for a good price, now they had more than enough funds for the new project.

They opted for a good-sized pool of fifty by twenty feet. The hot pool would go alongside the swimming pool together with a large storage room, so as not to add more length to the building.

Once all the cement was dry enough, Andrew busied himself with the walls of the building and the roof on top of it. It had him so busy, that he never was able to hike for over a month, but he was cheerful and always answered the children's questions. They wanted to know everything, of course.

Halge's knee was healed enough now that she could go on longer hikes and bike rides. She was encouraged by her husband to go on her own and with the children on weekends because he didn't want to interrupt his work.

At the end of July, the time for the big moment had arrived, to take a dip and a swim in their own pool. It was some event, to say it very mildly. "No more riding into town," Halge said overjoyed, "and... Oh, I love the hot pool."

The last thing Andrew had to do was nail on the roof covering of long metal sheets, easy to install. The solar collector panels already had been up for a month or so, to get the water hot.

Getta, one of the four ladies and a neighbor of the Herdens, was the first over and she simply couldn't say enough about their new addition. "I think I will have my own hot pool too. Now I understand you guys, driving so often into Duncan. Mind if I use your swimming pool once in a while?"

"Of course not," Halge said at once, "why don't you have a door in the fence and come in through the back door?"

That had the children thinking, and Floyd added, "Yes, then you can come in your bathing suit right away." She just grinned at the parents and thought, 'Children find everything so simple and easy. But they have a good point there...'

On the next rainy weekend, all their lady friends had come for a visit, and it was a hit with them as much. During a coffee and tea session, Halge asked, "I wonder how Hony is doing? Any of you heard from her?"

"I met her once in town," Mira replied, "and she looked like new. So happy, I tell you, she found the right man no doubt."

Hety then related, "By the way, we three had and still have an ad in the local paper and did get a lot of letters. So, there will be a lot of writing back and forth... We don't intend to meet a guy without knowing something about him."

Andrew commented, "I think you do the right thing. Let's face it, from nothing comes nothing. If you want a million dollars some day, you'll have to buy a lotto ticket once a week. It's that simple. It always comes to that. If we want the help of Spirit, we have to do our thing first. I think I mentioned it before."

Getta said at once, "But you have this special gift. Not everybody has that..."

"Fiddle, faddle, Getta," Andrew interrupted and looked sharply at her, "you're belittling yourself. We all have the very same potential within us, which is soul. With your kind of talk, you will discourage soul to help you. Besides," and he began to whisper, "Spirit is probably standing in the wings and laughing into It's fist because ninety-five percent of the world's population is in the very same bracket."

It had them all laughing and clapping their hands, the way he had said that. Cheering up, Getta said, "With you next door now, just looking over the fence will remind me." She slapped his held-up hand with a deep grin.

*   *   *

Chapter 12

Julia and more...

It was four thirty, early in the morning and, as so often, Andrew was awake already and reading with a dim bedside lamp. When he heard a quiet knock, he put the book away and walked to the door to see who it could be. It was Julia!

"I saw your light under the door," she whispered, "and thought I could have a talk with you."

He motioned her to follow him and the two went under the blanket of his bed, facing each other. Then he asked, "What woke this young lady up so early? It's not too serious?"

She was searching for the right words, then whispered, "Many of the kids in school are so often talking about sex and I think some of the older boys have sex with the girls. In my class we girls talk about it, but we don't know what to say to the boy if he asks us. You probably know about all this and can tell me... I mean, we cannot just have sex...?"

Andrew whispered back, "Your mother and I discussed it already whether we should tell you and what we should tell you. I'm sure glad you came to me, because I think you're old enough to know and certainly mature enough to know what it's all about, particularly since you began to have your period."

A moment later, he continued, "As you know already because TV is blaring it out often enough, sex has become a play of lust and power, a tool to get people around to something. Some of the advertisements are in that direction, by brainwashing people. Unfortunately, our society today is so often sex oriented, and the young people picking up on that, thinking it's OK to have sex for fun. In some schools in the States they even have condom machines, as if it was all right to have sex, but don't get pregnant. It's all backwards, Julia. It's all backwards.

"Thousands of years ago — as it is the case in the animal world — sex between a married couple was for the purpose to reproduce. But since then it has deteriorated, and to most of the people the meaning of sex has changed. Who am I to tell you now that sex is only for the purpose of having children? That is not valid anymore because people's consciousness has changed. We cannot go backward either in that respect.

"So, when and where does sex come into the picture or play — I don't know better words — when we have a loving partner. When we get married. Making love, another term for having sex, should never be without loving each other, or it just becomes lust, something rather empty to satisfy your mind, which will not last.

"I only know you for a short time, Julia, but the way you stuck with your mother at your father's

175

death, and the way you behave, tells me that you have a very strong character. You know what you want and are in control. And to come to me with this so often vital question of what sex is all about, tells me that you have trust in me, trust in us, your parents. It never will be broken because we also trust you."

After a moment, Julia put her arms around Andrew and held on for a long time. Then she kissed him and left the bed with, "Thank you, Andrew."

Halge just saw the back of her daughter, tip-toeing out of the bedroom. Snuggling up beside him in bed, she asked surprised, "What was all that about?"

He grinned, "For the last hour or so, we discussed a very important subject, but had to whisper, so as not to wake up a certain lady in her beauty sleep. Now I can speak louder and will tell you, my beloved."

* * *

The swimming pool went over big, of course, now finished, it gave Andrew also more time to plan for other hikes in the forest, away from the Duncan area. However, there was so much logging going on north of the Malahat Mountain, that he said one day, "I haven't been on an old logging road toward Oliphant Lake, and I think I shall explore that today whether it's still usable. If I have to get off the trail, I'm taking the cell phone and give you periodic reports. I don't know whether I'll be home for supper, so don't wait for me."

He parked his car at the end of a steep road, opposite a burned down house. Only a year ago, people still had been living there. But when they put the house up for sale and it was empty, somebody had set it on fire.

On his way, he soon discovered that the logging company had made a mess out of the old trail, now they had widened and graveled it, to be used by heavy trucks. When he heard the work of heavy equipment, he veered off into the forest, to bypass the active logging.

As Andrew was penetrating deeper and deeper into the woods, he gave Halge his first report, he said, "Oh darling, all the old trails are not what they used to be. We might as well forget doing anymore hiking around here. You know it was about here I met the five ladies last year. It was so nice and peaceful then. No, I don't like what they're doing to our forest. The old logging outfits were more considerate, but now... It seems to me that a lot of anger is manifesting, how to make a lot of profit. Well, I'll let you go now, my beloved." And he pocketed the cell phone again.

The noise of the heavy logging was in the far distance now, as he penetrated further into the often very thick forest. He thought, 'I'm glad the sun is out, it makes it rather easy to find your direction. And there I see the high tension lines way down below through an opening, meaning I'm walking parallel to it.'

During one of his stops, to see which way he wanted to go, Andrew thought that he heard voices. So he walked slowly into that direction, listening, waling and listening again. Through some dense bushes, he recognized a low structure, made out of evergreen branches. It was difficult to see. If it hadn't been for the voices, he never would've discovered it, it was so well camouflaged.

The voices coming to his ears, that of a woman and a man, seemed to be arguing, but not overly loud. Andrew thought, 'They're not too young, certainly no high school kids. They're speaking English, I don't think they're some terrorists...'

Then a third person, also a woman, began to participate in the argument, and she was louder. He could make out a sentence, "If you let us go..." The rest of the words were too quiet to understand. Then he heard a man say, "No way, no way!"

'What am I going to do?' the listener asked himself. 'Perhaps the women are held here against their will, but...' At that moment, he heard a voice behind him, "I suggest you hold up your hands, mister."

Looking around, Andrew saw a rifle pointed at him by a bearded young man in camouflaged clothing. He then said, "So you found us, hey? Too bad for you."

By now the other man had come out of the bunker-like housing, also holding a rifle at him. The first one said, "He was listening... You guys had to speak so loud, I could hear it a mile away. Now we have the two girls and this guy..." Then, "We better tie him up and decide with Fred later on, after he comes back."

Andrew was surprised over the roomy inside of the bunker. It was odd that they never searched or even addressed him with questions or anything of that nature. One of the men took his hands and put them on his back, where he tightened them with a rope. Then, after he pushed him into another room on the ground, he said, "We're like terrorists and don't mind killing or being killed, so you know what you're up to." With that he left.

Andrew thought, 'He speaks well... All this can mean only one thing, to them I'm already dead. They just wait until darkness when the forest is empty of the loggers and other human beings.'

There was still enough light coming in from the outside to make out the surroundings. It seemed that the two men had left the bunker, so Andrew stuck his head through the opening into the other room, where he saw the two women huddling together on the floor.

He did some quick thinking, then addressed them, and they were surprised to hear his voice, "Mind telling me what all this is about?"

One of them whispered, "They got us in here under false pretenses a week ago. We think they want to rape us, but they can't agree on anything. We tried to escape, but Fred with his dog found us again, then beat the hell out of us. We hardly know where we are... Now they try to figure out what to do with us. Fred probably will be back when it's dark with some food. We're already half starved."

"Where are they now?" Andrew asked.

"They always go to meet Fred up the mountain, where there's a big lake," one of them answered.

Suddenly Andrew had an idea and he pleaded with them, "Untie me at once. I know exactly where we are and will lead us three out of this forest quickly."

"But what about his dog?"

"Forget about the dog, this is our only chance. I have a bad feeling about them..." he urged them.

They undid his rope, but it took some doing. Then looking out of the entrance, Andrew didn't see any of the men, so he waved them to follow him with the words, "Follow me quickly, soon we'll be on a trail where we can walk and even run much faster."

Half of the trail was still under water, and Andrew thought, 'That might assist us... The dog can't get our scent in this water.'

He rushed them on and on, until they came to a logging road, newly done by the logging company. "Let's take a shortcut here through the bushes, where we wind up on another logging road." It all was easy for Andrew, but the ladies were struggling because their shoes were not made to walk in this wild forest.

Suddenly they could hear the dog barking in the distance. There was no doubt now that they were after them... Lamenting and complaining about their sore and hurt feet, Andrew rushed the two on, "Think what they will do to you!"

When they came to the former cement-haul road, he said, "In ten minutes we'll be at my car and safe, so let's not slow down now and get shot by those guys."

The barking of the dog had come very close when they entered Andrew's car. Zooming down the paved road, he laughed, "We've made it, girls... Now we'll call the police..."

"No, please," one of the women called out, "they're going to get us."

Stopping the car and looking back with a serious face, Andrew said, "You have been kidnapped and held for a week against your will, and now you want to forget it? Come on, you guys, you're not children, but adults..." Then, "Where are you from?"

With disdain, one of them answered, "From Victoria..."

"Well..." he wanted an answer, but they were quiet.

Driving again, he said, "You guys are crazy... You might not want to call the police, but I will. And I also will help them to find the three men. They even might be terrorists for all we know, and I have no love for them because they almost killed my wife. And they probably would've been taking care of me too, ha ha, but I'm still here..."

That reminded him, and while he had to stop at a light, turning onto the highway, he pulled out the cell phone, to tell his beloved wife why he was so late. It had begun to darken already. "I'll be home in ten or so minutes with two ladies. We're well and alive, at least I am. We're driving toward home. There I will tell you all."

"Oh, Andrew," Halge replied, "you don't know how we worried about you..."

"Yes, my beloved, I can imagine..."

As he turned into their home driveway, they all came rushing out, and the hugging went on and on.

Then turning to the ladies, Andrew said, "May I introduce... I don't even know your names..."

"I'm Doris," said one, "and this is Helen."

Walking toward the house, Andrew said, "I'm OK, but they both have very sore and burning feet. You'll find out why when I tell you the whole story."

Helen and Doris were occupying one of the bathrooms for the next hour or so, while the man of the house had something to eat first, and then he told his story, with Louise on his lap. At the end of the account he said, with a tone that wouldn't leave any doubt, "Tomorrow I shall lead the police to that place. Hopefully they're stupid enough and are still there. I shall not rest until they've caught them." Then, "Having the nerve to tie my wrists..."

It was late for the two little ones and they were ushered to bed, where their father said, "No stories tonight, you two. What I've told you was wild enough. So, sleep well and have some good dreams."

"I love you, Andrew," and they both gave him a kiss and a hug.

Coming out of the bathroom, Helen said, "It was very dumb of us, not wanting to go after them. We'll help the police, of course."

"And now you're hungry," Halge led them into the kitchen. "There's plenty of food, so help yourselves. You can sleep in the guest room, and in the morning, my husband will call the police. So do relax, if you can. Hopefully, your ordeal will be over now."

Doris said then, "I don't know how to thank you..." she addressed Andrew. "I mean the way you led us through the wild forest... the bushes..."

Andrew grinned, "It's part of my back yard, kind of. I know every part of that forest. How do you think I got there to begin with? I simply wanted to walk on one of my old trails again, which I hadn't done for over a year. Lo and behold, I was led on in this endeavor by an unseen force, my old friend Spirit. Who can doubt that?"

* * *

The RCMP (Royal Canadian Mounted Police) were all ears, and they finally realized the seriousness of this happening, and had three police cruisers with armed police officers lined up to go after the three men.

"I suggest we drive in from Spectacle Lake," Andrew proposed, "from there it's easier to find." The corporal in charge took his advice because they themselves hadn't a clue about the location of the bunker where it happened. They had a key to the gate across the road to Oliphant Lake, where they were able to park their cars.

They might've driven five minutes, when they encountered three men with a dog, one of them in camouflage clothing. The women being in the last car, recognized them at once and Helen called out, "That's them! I know Fred because he beat the hell out of me."

The police had stopped the cars and backed up again a short distance. The men did not try to run away. On the contrary, when they recognized the women, Fred called out, "We wondered where you had gone, girls. To our surprise, our place was empty."

Andrew had left the car and said, "What about me?" He had approached the group from the other side. Pretending to look puzzled, Fred said, "I don't know you, sir." Which was true, of course, but his two buddies also denied seeing him before. Obviously, all three were well-prepared for just this encounter and there was no way to prove anything.

"Where are your rifles?" asked one of the policemen.

"Oh, we always leave them in the cabin," Fred answered. He seemed to be their spokesman. "We never take them with us out here."

The corporal said then, "We will have to search

your cabin…"

"I can take you there," Fred tried to help out.

Pointing to Andrew, the Mounty replied, "We have a very capable man here. He knows where you cabin is located." Then, "I would appreciate if you three would stick around with one of our men until we're back. It shouldn't take too long."

"Of course, officer, we don't mind," he sounded cocky.

The two women had no intention of waiting out here with the three men, so they changed over to the second cruiser, to rather wait at Oliphant Lake with one of the policemen.

After they had left the cars, the policeman with the German Shepherd dog led the way along the first part of the trail — probably a former logging road — and it was easy enough to see. But at the turn-off toward a look-out on top of a huge rock, Andrew suggested, "I'll mark the trail from here with this blue ribbon for you, so you'll be able to find it later on. I always carry some ribbon in my pocket."

They made good headway through light bushes and in fifteen minutes had reached what the men had called a cabin. While Andrew waited outside, three of the policemen entered the half-underground bunker. Soon they came out again, not having found anything of importance. Their rifles had not been hidden away.

Andrew said, "I'm sorry, gentlemen, but something doesn't seem right here…" He did not want to say what his intuition was telling him. After all, they were policemen, looking for proof and facts.

Then he said, "I wonder where their outhouse is?"

So the dog handler prodded the dog to look. They came to a primitive sitting arrangement with no roof over the top, and that's when the dog really got excited, barking down into the pit of excrement. "I think we've got something here," the policeman called out. "They might've buried something in that shit."

One of the policemen got some plastic bags out of his backpack and slipped them over his legs, to make sure that none of that grime would get on his pants. They had found a spade at the bunker, and with it he began to probe into the stinky excrement. Although it was not too deep, he already had sunk up to his knees into the stuff.

When he felt something solid rather, he tried to fish it out with the spade... It was a human leg! He called out, "Give me a rope, the shit is getting too deep and I want to tie the rope around the leg."

Out of the pit again, he used some evergreen boughs to wipe some of the grime off his legs, while the other policemen pulled a woman's body out of the pit... She was still was dressed. The courageous policeman went into the smelling hell once more, and out they fished a second woman's body.

"We'll leave them right here," the corporal said. "Our lab people can do the rest," he shook himself in disgust. "Now we'll have those guys for good."

On their way back again, he said to Andrew, "Those two girls up there can thank you, or they might've wound up in the same pit..." He didn't finish the sentence.

Before they had reached their cars again, the policeman said once more, "Don't tell the girls yet, they might give us away. We want to shackle them first, and make sure they're not running away."

The surprise was complete, when the Mounties put handcuffs on the three men. The corporate said, "You can safe your breath. We found the bodies in your toilet pit."

The three were crammed onto the back seat of one of the cruisers, with two policemen riding in the front. All others and the dog occupied the other two cars, except two policemen, who would be picked up later on, because of the limited room.

They were on their way to the Duncan police headquarters. Andrew had phoned Halge to give her an idea, and then said, "They want me to come with them to record everything. It might take some time. Give my kisses to the children, and maybe we shouldn't tell them, hey?"

*   *   *

Andrew offered his help once more when he said to the sergeant at headquarters, "By the way, there's a much shorter way to the sight of the bunker, and I'm willing to show it to you."

The next day they called on him, but this time he took his own car also. He didn't feel like sticking around until all their investigation had been completed. And then they still had to carry out the bodies.

At home again, Andrew said to Halge, "We only see the police doing their job on the highway. I wouldn't want to be in their shoes doing this dirty work."

However, this was not the end of the story... Somehow, the news media got hold of Andrew's name and found out where he lived. For days the Herdens had to put up with the very pesky men and women of the press and TV, but they tried not to loose their cool, because Andrew had prepared them with, "If we get angry, they'll really go after us. So let me do most of the talking and just point to me."

Unfortunately, this also revealed to Louise and Floyd the terrible happening at the hidden forest bunker, and not to forget their father's own involvement. It was unavoidable. When they were on their own, Andrew commented to Halge, "You want to bring up the children a certain way and this comes along. Well, at least we still have them under our roof for a while."

* * *

When the adults were sitting in the living room, while Louise and Floyd played outside with their friends and Julia was upstairs in her room doing homework, Halge started a conversation with, "Julia is maturing rapidly since the time she got her period one and a half years back. There's so much now she wants to know, as if she's going into life in a month or two. The way she was following the trial of the three men who murdered the women. She simply wants to know everything." Andrew just nodded.

A bit later, she continued, "Since those press people invaded our privacy and came up with all kinds of questions, even our little ones — I don't know why I still call them 'little ones', because they also have matured a lot — even Louise and Floyd are quite sure that you saved the other two women, and they're proud that it was their father who did it."

Then, "I can't help it, Andrew, with this terrible happening. Although it was so negative, there's a positive change in the three and they want more answers ... but they don't quite know what to ask."

Nodding, Andrew replied, "Yes, you put it very well. It probably is soul behind the scenes, prodding... Soul, already matured, is trying to contact the intellect in a child, but the intellect is not yet matured enough to grasp. It's a small revolution in every youngster growing up. The thing is, however, that we parents give them a secure life and proper guidance, so that the growth in our children is not hampered with some disadvantage. Their trust in us is so important, and that we trust them."

"The way you put that, my beloved," she sat down beside him, "you're a perfect father. That's why Julia comes to you. Instinctively she knows that you can give her the answer and be of help. But I'm not jealous. How could I...? Our love does not tolerate it."

"To change the subject," Andrew began, "I read the book about Frederick the Great. There's a lot in there for the German ego to love, and they still see him as the great person today. And, of course, Hitler saw himself in that greatness."

Then, "However, by today's standards, by today's stage of consciousness of the sane populous of our Earth, I don't see any greatness in Frederick the II who used wars to get his way. On one side he tried to help his people by putting in all kinds of reforms. On the other side he went to war to gain property, and his soldiers were slaughtered by the thousands."

He finished it with the words, "It's a pity and sad that many Germans, like our German driver, Fritz, still see him as a great man to this day."

Two days later, Julia approached Andrew with the words, "I kind of wonder, Andrew, about the two women who were murdered, but also the two you met at the bunker. I know you refuse to be told that you saved them. I understand that because if it wasn't for them, you probably never would've gotten the rope off your wrists. So, it can go both ways."

He nodded, "Smart thinking, Julia, not that your little siblings will believe it. That's where maturity comes in and the ability to discriminate," he gave her a pat on the arm.

"But that's not what I want to speak about," she continued. "It's about those women... How come they followed those men, to begin with?"

"There're so many factors, Julia," he held her hand. "What kind of women were they and are they? We ask ourselves the question. It often starts with the parents. Was there love in the parents' marriage? Was there only one parent that had to work without having the time to look after the child? Did they watch TV at every opportunity? And later on in high school, you know yourself that not all girls are strong enough to live a so-called clean life, often not even know the meaning of it.

"If those women had been taught," he said once more, "the meaning of discrimination and how to apply it properly — as your mother and myself at every opportunity mention and teach — they never would've followed those men. Does one need hard experience to know? Of course not. Experiences are good, but do we have to take drugs to prove to ourselves that they're bad? You see how important it is to have a good beginning. And that's what your mother and I want to give you, to be ready for life and to face every emergency."

Then he said, "And I only spoke of the physical

aspects of our lives. We also teach you about the Law of Cause and Effect and Karma. Not many people go by that or even have heard about them. Why are we put into a certain body? Because we haven't learned a certain lesson in a former lifetime. It's a vast subject, Julia, and we will speak about it many times more. There are so many things we still don't know, but we already have a good beginning."

A bit later, he finally said, "Let there be Spirit in your life, Julia, and listen to your intuition, soul. They're the tools of God."

Her arms flew around him, and she whispered, "Thank you so much, Andrew." Then she asked rather haltingly, "You think I could call you Dad and father? Louise brought it up actually. They also want to call you that."

With tears in his eyes, he replied, giving her a big squeeze, "I would like nothing better, my daughter."

* * *

Epilogue of
Let There Be Love

More and more the world of man is subjected to violence and of late terrorism, and one begins to wonder, is this the beginning of a new war?

If man would adhere and, to begin with, believe in the existence of Spirit, he would find protection and, perhaps also, love through this voice of God.

Unfortunately though, the majority of our western world populous, think and pray to their God during an emergency only, as if It was merely available part time.

Soul, made of the very same material as that of Spirit and God, is in every one of us... Our intuition is soul or Spirit trying to speak to us. A woman's intuition... In general, women are more endowed with this voice of Spirit, and they will listen to It.

However, the foregoing does not fit too well into man's life of power and vanity.

Perhaps this story of *Let There Be Love* will help to open man's consciousness to the superior force of Spirit, and mellow him in his relationship with the opposite sex...

Spirit will do wonders, helping in all of our affairs. Are we willing to listen?

E N D

ISBN 141200120-X